A NOVEL BASED ON THE LIFE OF
LUCA PACIOLI

THE
DIVINE
PROPORTIONS
OF
LUCA PACIOLI

W. A. W. Parker

THE **M** MENTORIS PROJECT

Barbera Foundation, Inc.
P.O. Box 1019
Temple City, CA 91780

Copyright © 2019 Barbera Foundation, Inc.
Front cover photo: Sheila Terry / Science Photo Library
Back cover photo: Science History Images / Alamy Stock Photo
Cover design: Suzanne Turpin

More information at www.mentorisproject.org

ISBN: 978-1-947431-27-0

Library of Congress Control Number: 2019937843

All net proceeds from the sale of this book will be donated to Barbera Foundation, Inc. whose mission is to support educational initiatives that foster an appreciation of history and culture to encourage and inspire young people to create a stronger future.

The Mentoris Project is a series of novels and biographies about the lives of great Italians and Italian-Americans: men and women who have changed history through their contributions as scientists, inventors, explorers, thinkers, and creators. The Barbera Foundation sponsors this series in the hope that, like a mentor, each book will inspire the reader to discover how she or he can make a positive contribution to society.

Contents

Foreword   i

Dedication   1

Chapter One: The Battle of the Stones   3

Chapter Two: The Beans   9

Chapter Three: Education   13

Chapter Four: The Apprentice   19

Chapter Five: The Altar   25

Chapter Six: The Resurrection   29

Chapter Seven: Perspective   33

Chapter Eight: Sight   39

Chapter Nine: The Library   43

Chapter Ten: The Court of Earthly Delights   51

Chapter Eleven: The Wait   57

Chapter Twelve: O Sea   61

Chapter Thirteen: The Merchant of Venice   63

Chapter Fourteen: A New Language   65

Chapter Fifteen: The Cipher   69

Chapter Sixteen: When in Rome   73

Chapter Seventeen: The Conclave   79

Chapter Eighteen: Finding Alberti   83

Chapter Nineteen: Two Paintings   87

Chapter Twenty: Brothers   91

Chapter Twenty-One: The First   93

Chapter Twenty-Two: The Flower of the World   101

Chapter Twenty-Three: Guidobaldo   109

Chapter Twenty-Four: Round Two   115

Chapter Twenty-Five: The Rebirth   119

Chapter Twenty-Six: The Sum   121
Chapter Twenty-Seven: The Fine Print   125
Chapter Twenty-Eight: On Computing   127
Chapter Twenty-Nine: The Reception   133
Chapter Thirty: The New Athens   137
Chapter Thirty-One: The First Supper   141
Chapter Thirty-Two: The Last Supper   143
Chapter Thirty-Three: Divine Inspiration   149
Chapter Thirty-Four: The Irrational Collaboration   153
Chapter Thirty-Five: The Horse   157
Chapter Thirty-Six: The Escape   159
Chapter Thirty-Seven: Begone Dull Care   161
Chapter Thirty-Eight: The Next Move   169
Chapter Thirty-Nine: The Wall   177
Chapter Forty: The Ouster   179
Chapter Forty-One: Where There's Smoke . . .   181
Chapter Forty-Two: The Rumor   183
Chapter Forty-Three: Twenty-Six Days Later   185
Chapter Forty-Four: The Betrayal   189
Chapter Forty-Five: Just the Two of Us   193
Chapter Forty-Six: The Reprint   197
Chapter Forty-Seven: On the Game of Chess   199
Chapter Forty-Eight: The Quantitative Strength   203
Chapter Forty-Nine: The Vitruvian Man   211
Chapter Fifty: Proportion and Proportionality   213
Chapter Fifty-One: The Printing Pressure   219
Chapter Fifty-Two: The Monastery   223
Chapter Fifty-Three: Will and Testament   229
Chapter Fifty-Four: The Last Days   233
Chapter Fifty-Five: The Divine Proportions   235
About the Author   239

Foreword

First and foremost, Mentor was a person. We tend to think of the word *mentor* as a noun (a mentor) or a verb (to mentor), but there is a very human dimension embedded in the term. Mentor appears in Homer's *Odyssey* as the old friend entrusted to care for Odysseus's household and his son Telemachus during the Trojan War. When years pass and Telemachus sets out to search for his missing father, the goddess Athena assumes the form of Mentor to accompany him. The human being welcomes a human form for counsel. From its very origins, becoming a mentor is a transcendent act; it carries with it something of the holy.

The Barbera Foundation's Mentoris Project sets out on an Athena-like mission: We hope the books that form this series will be an inspiration to all those who are seekers, to those of the twenty-first century who are on their own odysseys, trying to find enduring principles that will guide them to a spiritual home. The stories that comprise the series are all deeply human. These books dramatize the lives of great Italians and Italian-Americans whose stories bridge the ancient and the modern, taking many forms, just as Athena did, but always holding up a light for those living today.

Whether in novel form or traditional biography, these

books plumb the individual characters of our heroes' journeys. The power of storytelling has always been to envelop the reader in a vivid and continuous dream, and to forge a link with the subject. Our goal is for that link to guide the reader home with a new inspiration.

What is a mentor? A guide, a moral compass, an inspiration. A friend who points you toward true north. We hope that the Mentoris Project will become that friend, and it will help us all transcend our daily lives with something that can only be called holy.

—Robert J. Barbera, President, Barbera Foundation
—Ken LaZebnik, Editor, The Mentoris Project

Dedication

Although I've spent much time as a friar contemplating the afterlife, it seems my own death has crept up on me. I am no longer capable of writing myself. I can no longer put pen to paper. I can no longer produce the quick flick of a pen and the sound it makes as it scrapes the page. I miss feeling fully in charge of the words about to spring forth from my quill. I miss the moments where I feel completely lost, milling about in a dark valley, only to suddenly hear a siren atop a hill beckoning me to the light.

But it is not to be. I am weak and bedridden. Now, I can only speak the words I wish to write. Luckily, my good fortune has given me a young friar on his novitiate to transcribe my words, the very same you are reading now. Though luck doesn't have too much to play into the current situation since I am the head of the monastery where he and I reside. I gave the charge for him to sit at my bedside myself, but I do consider it lucky to be in the position to make such a charge.

As with most of my books, I am dedicating this one to you, my students. I wish I had taken the time during Alberti or Piero's last days, as I am now making this young man do, and sat down to receive their final wisdom. Hopefully, when we are done, there will still be enough time to take out all the stuffy language

I'm sure to employ and make it much more enjoyable to read. I have spent the majority of my life writing books for you. Books on mathematics, bookkeeping, the divine proportion, and how to apply these fields to the real world. You will probably find most of them to be better written than this one will be. But in all of them I never explained what motivated me to write so many tomes. May this book show you my inspiration so that when you surpass me, and hopefully soon, I may still be able to inspire others, guiding them to surpass you in turn.

—Luca Pacioli

Chapter One

THE BATTLE OF THE STONES

All of my earliest memories are of trying to sneak out of the house. In all but one, my mother catches me red-handed as I endeavor to slip out the back door or shimmy through a window. I always had one purpose in mind: I wanted to see the Battle of the Stones. In this desire I was not alone in my household. My father went to the game regularly, as did my brother, Piero. This is not the same Piero I mentioned in the dedication, but a lovely man nonetheless. My brother Piero was older than me and already had two boys around my age. And he had just started allowing them to come to the game with him. I was determined that I must be allowed to follow suit. Unfortunately, my mother had another plan in mind. She forbade me from going.

This made me angry, so angry that I could shout. And I often did. I find it cathartic now, looking back on how much the devil was in me in those days, and how much I've purged him from my life since then.

I would plead my case to her, however flimsy it must have been, but she remained steadfast. She never replied to any of my protestations. She would simply say, "Miracles can be undone." Her stoicism made me so angry. Many years later I learned she had a series of miscarriages between Piero's birth and mine, but that had no bearing on my behavior at the time.

When I was five or six, I came up with a brilliant scheme. I would do all of my daily chores early in the morning, after the rooster but before the sun. The floors would be spotless. The dishes shiny, practically new. She would surely have to let me go under those conditions, no? But alas, the answer was still no. I tried this strategy many times, each time hoping I would get into her good graces and gain her permission, to no avail.

One morning I finished my chores much sooner than usual, even before the rooster. As my mother had not roused yet I had no one to plead with. In that hour, I saw my escape. On game days I would normally be there when she awoke, ready to pester her for her permission. But this morning, I made sure that she found me still in bed, or rather back in bed, having convinced her that I must have fallen back to sleep after doing my chores so early. I lay still with my eyes shut. Although I was quiet, my mind was not. My thoughts raced: What do people do when they're asleep? Should I keep breathing or hold my breath? My father makes loud grating noises like a pig that has found a truffle, should I?

I can only imagine my mother must have been relieved to find me sleeping, not having to endure my onslaught that day. She didn't stay long to ponder my con, though. As soon as she left my bedroom I bolted upright and stealthily crept out of the house unmolested.

I had done it.

My feet flew fast on the cobblestones through town. I didn't chance looking back in case my mother was closing in. I ran through the Piazza San Francesco, weaving through trees all the way past the Cathedral as the sun started peeking over the horizon. I knew the game was played just beyond the city gate.

The stone archway amplified the roar of the crowd as I passed through. It was like they were cheering me on, welcoming me to the game.

Nearly breathless, I poked my head between the spectators on the sidelines. I couldn't wait to see it. My eager eyes peered onto the field, but all I could see was grass. Was I too late? Was it over? In my panic, I realized that although I had a deep desire to go to the game, I had no idea what it actually entailed. Could this be the game? Standing in a field and yelling?

But no, everyone was cheering, their gazes fixed on the far end of the field. What were they looking at? I could make out some fuzzy shapes darting around, but not much more. Could they see that far? It was hard to imagine they could. I had no concept that my sight was limited. And my ears did me no good either. Any noise the shapes were making was muffled by the screaming men around me.

Suddenly, a loud crack rose above the din, followed by a mix of exhilarated and disgusted outbursts from the crowd. Then the shapes became clearer, turning into men. They raced toward each other. Some carried shields. Some breastplates and others deerskin stockings. One resplendent gentleman wore a helmet in the shape of a sparrow hawk's head. Although the men all wore all kinds of different garb, they each carried the same accessory: a rock.

Stones littered the air. Men were falling fast. The man with the sparrow hawk's helmet ran out in front of the pack, raised his stone to the heavens, and was unceremoniously smashed in the face. Another man's stone had halted his own. I think the man fell to the ground, but all I remember seeing is his blood flying through the air. Some of it hit an old man near me in the face. To my surprise, the old man wiped the red stain from his brow, smiled and then ran out onto the field. He grabbed a fallen man's shield and smacked another man with it. He was not disturbed by the blood that struck him, rather it seemed to excite something disturbed within him.

Some of the man's blood landed on my shirt too, but it did not propel me toward bloodlust. Rather, it spurred in me a deep dread. If my mother wasn't going to be mad at me for sneaking out to the game, she surely would be now.

When I looked up, there was a big brawl in front of me, a free-for-all of violence and gore. The two sides hurled stones at one another with increasing ferocity. Amongst all this chaos, I noticed the lithe young man was lying on the ground, motionless. Indeed, he had fallen. Although I had never seen a dead body before, I knew this was my first.

Shouts of "Halt!" and "Stop!" arose from the crowd. A couple of men went to the young man, checked to see if he was breathing, and then dragged his body off the field.

His corpse had only just been removed when the two sides commenced bludgeoning each other. The game had begun again as quickly as it had ceased, with scant recognition of the life lost.

I turned to a woman beside me, "That's not the end of it?"

"That's just the first part, dear."

I had seen enough.

I ran.

Tears filled my eyes. I was used to not seeing far, but the tears made it hard to see anything around me. I stumbled through the stone archway that seemed to welcome me to the game. Now it ricocheted my sobs back at me, taunting me.

I would find out later that the point of the Battle of the Stones was to hold the area in the middle of the field long enough to gain undisputed possession of it. Six years before my birth, the Battle of Anghiari between Florence and Milan gave Florence undisputed control over Sansepulcro, my village. I can't imagine it was much of a battle. Who would want to fight for control of my remote little rock in the middle of nowhere? Perhaps for that reason, Florence and Milan hadn't fought very vigorously for it. Only one man died in the Battle of Anghiari and that man fell off his horse as his regiment got into formation.

The Battle of the Stones was different. My neighbors relished murdering each other. There was no control at stake beyond the temporary occupation of a patch of grass. The Battle of the Stones was brutal and pointless. How could we do this to one another?

I cried thinking of the man in the sparrow hawk's helmet. I wanted to run back to my mother's arms, but I couldn't go home, at least not yet. My mother would still be angry at me this early after my treachery and she might stone me if I came back before her anger abated.

I didn't want people on the street to see me crying, though. I needed to find a place to hide.

0

Transcriber's note: Fra. Luca Pacioli was adamant that I finish each chapter with a number, in order, from the Fibonacci sequence (0, 1, 1, 2, 3, 5, 8, 13, 21, 34, etc). I have done so, in that mode.

Chapter Two

THE BEANS

My cheeks were still wet as I wandered into the Cathedral. Brother Angelo, one of the younger priests, greeted me cheerfully.

"Luca!"

I'm sure he saw the blood on my shirt and the shiny patches of tears on my cheeks. His tone shifted, but he tactfully sidestepped confronting me about it directly.

"Where's your mother?" he asked.

"I'm sure she'll be along soon."

My plan was to wait for my mother at the church. She was a pious woman who came to church every day after her morning chores. I usually came with her and I was hoping to convince her I came early to sneak in a few prayers before the main service. My plan was to charm her with feigned piety and I was pretty sure it was going to work. I didn't have an excuse for the blood on my shirt yet, but there was still time.

Brother Angelo smiled weakly. "Well. It's good to have as many souls as we can during Stones season."

I looked around the nave. Only a handful of people occupied the pews. Although I wanted to distance myself from the proceeding across town, the relative lack of attendance infuriated me.

"Why does everyone watch them kill each other like that?"

This seemed to strike a nerve in Brother Angelo. He corrected me, "Am I there? Are all these good people there?"

"No."

"Well. That's not everyone, is it?"

I should have let his words be the last of it, but that was not in my youthful nature.

"Everyone else in town was there!" I screamed.

The handful of parishioners snapped their heads around and stared at me.

Brother Angelo should have put my insolence on display. He should have slapped me across the face and kicked me out of His church. But he bent down and carefully took my shoulder in his hand.

"I know the Battle of the Stones is popular, but our town is full of good people."

But a majority of them had just seen a man murdered and then gleefully cheered the proceeding on, ravenous for the next victim! Sansepulcro was a bad place full of bad people and I needed to prove this to Brother Angelo. I just needed to show him that the town was hungrier for blood than Scripture. To prove it, undeniably in my mind, I only needed two numbers: One, the population of Sansepulcro and two, the number in attendance at that barbaric enterprise.

Brother Angelo wouldn't know the latter number so I told myself I would have to swallow hard, go back and count them myself. I couldn't do much with numbers in those days, but I could count and that savage spectacle was probably still underway.

I was sure Brother Angelo would have the first number.

"How many people live in Sansepulcro?"

"I don't know."

"What do you mean you don't know? Who does?"

Again, Brother Angelo demonstrated his supreme grace. "No one does, but we do keep a record of the baptisms we perform."

"How many is that?"

"Let me show you."

He led me over to the baptismal font where he produced a large, ornate wooden box. I was curious. Why do they keep this number in a box? Brother Angelo tilted the box toward me. Whatever I was expecting, nothing prepared me for what was inside.

"Beans?"

"For every baby baptized we add one to it. Black beans for boys and white beans for girls."

"And how many are there?"

"You can count them if you like."

The enormity of the undertaking overwhelmed me. The box was almost half as large as I was. Regardless, I knew that I had to convince Brother Angelo of Sansepulcro's irredeemability. I started counting furiously. Beans flew through my fingers. I decided to place the beans in piles of one hundred. I was making quick work of the task, but then the image of the dead man in the sparrow hawk's helmet flashed before my eyes. For some reason, this tempered the intensity with which I was counting and made me wonder something.

"If someone dies. Do you take their bean away?"

"No. This is a record of life, not death," Brother Angelo answered.

A record of life! But this was no record of the souls alive in Sansepulcro. It was no record of the population. It was a record of acts. And not even acts that could be translated into the actual information I was seeking. The Black Death had killed off so many of my fellow citizens, perhaps more than the Stones, making this endeavor nowhere near remotely useful. And that wasn't even taking into account those that had died of natural causes.

So, while Brother Angelo's statement was poignant in its rudimentary simplicity, it meant that I wouldn't be able to prove my point. Since they don't take a bean away when someone died, there was no way to get an accurate count of the city's population. It probably wouldn't have mattered anyway. I wouldn't have been able to get through all the beans before my mother arrived. She was going to kill me for sneaking out, further altering the final count.

I slunk into a pew to await my fate. It was sure to arrive soon along with my mother. My mind raced, anxious to ascertain all the new chores she was sure to conjure as punishment.

But mostly, I thought about the beans.

1

Chapter Three

EDUCATION

I wondered if I would learn a better way than the beans in school. Even if I had the two numbers I wanted, I wouldn't have been able to do much with them. The monastery, the same one we're in right now, provided schooling to all the local boys free of charge. This was good because if they had charged, my family wouldn't have been able to afford it. I had always been aware of the two sides of the "poor, but respectable" label my family had. More often than not it meant that people thought less of you, but didn't want to say so to your face. My family's poverty felt like it was emblazoned on the small of my back, something I could never scratch or rub off.

I couldn't have been more excited for my first day. Even the rich boys went here. We were going to learn arithmetic, geometry, bookkeeping, reading, grammar, and theology. Brother Carlo taught arithmetic. He was a rotund man who looked like drawings I had seen of the Ottoman conqueror Sultan Mehmet II, the one that had just taken Constantinople.

I wanted to learn how to use an abacus. I always went shopping with my mother so I could see the merchants use them to make calculations. It was a dazzling trick, moving the beads back and forth on the rods. It looked like magic. Everyone referred to my school as an "abacco" school so I was sure it was going to be the first thing we would learn, but my eagerness got the best of me. My hand was high in the air in Brother Carlo's classroom.

I didn't even let him begin lecturing before I asked, "When are we going to learn the abacus?"

"We won't. It's an outdated tool."

"But isn't this an *abacco* school?"

"Yes. But abacco doesn't mean abacus. It's the *modo Arabico*, the Arabic style. I will teach you a method of calculation that makes the abacus redundant."

I could feel the rich boys looking at me. Surely, they had already known this. My blood was boiling, ready to explode like a volcano. I was so embarrassed, but Brother Carlo's next words plugged up any potential eruption. His words were just so fascinating.

He explained that abacco allows for the addition, subtraction, multiplication, and division of Hindu-Arabic numbers (1, 2, 3 . . .) instead of roman ones (I, II, III, IV . . .). You use a pen and paper instead of an abacus. This allows you to see and keep track of the work you've done, whereas with an abacus there's no trace of the calculation made.

He explained, "God shows us His work. A tree does not just appear fully formed, strong roots, and wide branches. It grows from a seed and sapling. And we will show Him our work, too."

This made complete sense to me, but I tended not to follow the dictum. Brother Carlo routinely marked me down for not showing my work. We hadn't progressed far in our education at the time and were still doing simple, double-digit addition and subtraction. I didn't need to show my work. I didn't need a pen and paper to make the calculation. I could do it in my head.

He had us play a game. He would list a problem and we, the pupils, would calculate it. The first person with the correct answer won. Now, this was a game I could win. One day, he became particularly irate with me. The rules were that you had to show the work of the calculation before giving the answer, but that wasn't a rule I tended to follow, often merely making a show of putting pen to paper. On this day though, I made no such show, never even lowering my head or blotting my page with ink. I merely proclaimed the answer a second or two after he read the problem. And I was very smug about it.

So, Brother Carlo, in his wisdom, announced that we would have only one more problem that day. He said that the person who solved it by the end of class would never have to come back again. Clearly, they wouldn't have anything to learn.

This proposition excited me. Not because I wanted to be let out of arithmetic. I rather liked the class. It was the only place where I felt truly confident and it gave me an opportunity to demonstrate my burgeoning capability. I was, though, a bit too confident for how little I had actually advanced in my studies, at least in relation to my current position. Nevertheless, I told myself that I'd be gracious in victory. I would not embarrass Brother Carlo by not attending his lectures. I would remain a fixture in the class and continue to hold court there amongst the other students.

Then Brother Carlo recited the problem: 225,851,433,717 divided by 14,503.

I was fortunate that he read it aloud twice since my hand

wasn't even on my pen when he began. I had to scramble and barely got the numbers down the second time around. But that didn't do me much good. We had not yet learned division. I was aware of the basic concept, but these numbers were far beyond my grasp.

I didn't even know where to start. I didn't know how to divide. I only knew addition and subtraction. How could I be expected to solve this problem? But then I realized: I know addition and subtraction. And in a way, division is kind of like addition, only backwards and multiplied. While I didn't yet know how to actually go about dividing numbers, I thought maybe . . . if I added up 14,503 enough times I would get to the answer that way. Since it was my only course of action, I launched into it with zeal.

But I was so out of practice showing my work for addition that I struggled and sweated my way through the first few rounds. I could have sworn there was more sweat on that page than ink. And time was running out. The numbers simply weren't adding up fast enough to reach 225,851,433,717.

And then class was over. I looked around and noticed that I was the only student who had seriously attempted to solve it. Or perhaps they had known all along that I was the sole intended recipient of this rebuke. Either way, my fellow students filed out of the room expressing their disappointment at having to attend another arithmetic class.

Brother Carlo came over to my desk. He could see my disappointment, both on my face and on my page. I had drawn large, dramatic Xs over the work I had done. I expected his scorn, but was blessed with his scrutiny.

"Trying to solve the problem using addition. Hm. Impressive."

For a moment I thought I would be praised, but I was soon corrected.

"It wouldn't have worked, but it might have under the right conditions. But let's say it did. Could you have done this in your head?"

"No."

"Even if you could, if you made a mistake in your calculation, would you know how to fix it?"

"No."

"You wouldn't know where the problem was so you'd have to start all over again. You have to put in the work to achieve the result. Sometimes we face big problems and the only way we can get around them is to figure out where we went wrong and change course."

I knew he was talking about the problem, but also about my behavior. I was humiliated, but it had the desired result. I always showed my work from then on. My ego took a bruising that day, but it was soon massaged when I kept winning the calculation game.

Brother Carlo was a great teacher. But the friars taught no subject better than theology. I loved hearing about St. Francis, who had mentored a young Brother Angelo into the Order in Sansepulcro. This was, of course, a different Brother Angelo than the one who showed me the beans since it was over two hundred years ago. Or else Brother Angelo had decided not to be bound by the ravages of time.

St. Francis taught Brother Angelo a lesson about underestimating people. Three out-of-luck brigands sought bread at the monastery and Brother Angelo turned them away. But when St. Francis offered them bread, the men used the opportunity to redeem themselves and convert to Christianity.

I was about to be confirmed in the Church myself and so this story was a revelation. I wanted to change the course of my life, too, and shed my "poor, but respectable" label, the one that others automatically placed upon me without giving me a chance to redeem myself. The Church and my education could help me do that. I just had to put in the work.

1

Chapter Four

THE APPRENTICE

Not far into my education I would be able to divide those numbers. We learned division, multiplication, algebra and geometry. Each was a new language and my tongue was wet to learn them. I enjoyed school greatly. I could solve problems I'd never even heard of before.

School was my solace when the Black Death came to Sansepulcro. Its call was so deafening my parents had no choice but to answer it. As soon as my mother ran a fever she bid me stay away from them. But it was my father who died first. Mother held on for a couple days and then passed away. I was twelve years old. I don't know why, but I didn't inform my older brother Piero or the local authorities of their passing for a few days. I spent almost a week roaming about the house. I stuck to my chore schedule. The floors had never been shinier. The dishes were almost scraped clean of their luster. I didn't want anyone to know. I thought it might pass, like a bad dream. But it did not. It was a nightmare that still rouses me from my sleep to this day, despite the fact that it happened years ago. It was a painful occasion that I'd prefer not to speak about in further detail.

Piero tried to take my mind off the matters at hand by focusing my attention on my upcoming apprenticeship. While I didn't have to pay the friars anything for my education, it was common for an apprentice's family to pay a master for their training. But since my parents left neither Piero nor I with an inheritance, I could not afford to do so.

Luckily, Piero was able to arrange an apprenticeship with the businessman Folco de Belfolci. I would live with Folco, too. Since I couldn't pay him anything up front, I would not receive any wages later on in my training, as I would have customarily. It was a necessary arrangement, but one that also taught me perhaps the most important lesson of my apprenticeship: "Free" is not all that it seems.

Folco sold fabric, buttons, and thread. On my first visit it was apparent that both he and his shop had seen better times. Although the shop was not large, maybe the size of my family's old living room, it was sparsely populated with product. There were only a handful of reams lining the walls and they looked as decrepit as their shop owner. The musty smell of mold and death seemed to permeate everything, including Folco's breath. I still remember that first morning when Folco showed me how he kept his books. He used a daybook ledger, recording everything that happened in the shop. It was a simple narrative in a single column. This happened, then this happened, etc.

I was surprised to see that he still used roman numerals. "Why?" I asked him.

"I don't trust those Arab numbers. The Turks ruined Constantinople. They destroyed Christendom and they took away my fabrics. You see how many reams I have left? No alum means no fabric, means no business."

Later, I would learn that alum was a mordant for dyes. Alum makes it so that dyes don't run when the fabric is washed. The only alum mines were near Constantinople so when the city fell, the fabric trade in Italy was ruined. And Folco along with it.

Folco went on. "Those Arabs are shifty and so are their numbers."

Folco grabbed the daybook ledger. He wrote the numeral six in it and then added a small line, turning the six into an eight. He was proud of his example. Even though it was my first day, I couldn't help but interject.

"You can easily notice that the number's been changed since it's not two circles, one on top of the other. The proportion is off."

Folco began grumbling. It was the sort of low, indecipherable grumble that I would come to ignore. He grabbed the daybook ledger and changed a numeral one to a numeral four. I could have given it to him. It was a great example. But I didn't.

"You can manipulate roman ones, too."

I changed a III to an VIII in the daybook ledger, and then a X to an IX.

"And that's only the beginning," I said in the smug tone I still hadn't learned to get rid of.

At this, Folco became frustrated and changed the subject. "We need to count the buttons! Here, you can use this."

He handed me an abacus.

"I'm sorry. I don't know how to use an abacus."

"What do they teach you at that school? First they forgot to teach you manners and now math."

"I promise I can add up any sum you can muster."

Folco grumbled. He gave me a list. He had already counted the numbers of the various types of buttons he had. He wanted to know how many buttons total were in his shop. It was a relatively straightforward problem. I did it in my head quickly, but put the calculation in the ledger to show my work since I had long been in the habit of doing so.

I displayed my work to Folco.

"This way you can see all the numbers and how they add up. And, if you make a mistake it's easier to see where you went wrong. With an abacus you wouldn't know what happened."

"You're my apprentice! Your job is to learn the way I do things! Watch closely."

Folco seized his abacus and grumbled his way through the calculation. He tried to pause at certain intervals to explain why he was doing what he was doing, but he used no words to explain his actions, his face simultaneously galled at having to show me such a simple procedure and fretful that he might lose his place in the calculation.

It may, therefore, come as no surprise that Folco's calculation was wrong. But as is the case with many such people, he didn't know that. He proudly announced the difference between our results as proof that I had no idea what I was doing and made me update the ledger to his erroneous outcome. Later, I updated the ledger to the correct number when he wasn't looking. I was nothing if not a dedicated apprentice. I didn't want his failings to lead to that of the shop and ultimately my own.

In a way, I remember that day fondly. I finally got to learn how to use an abacus. Despite Folco's inept teaching style, I got the gist of how to move the beads back and forth on the rods, breaking the rows into multiples of 10. It was elegant in its own, outmoded way. I'd go into more detail about how to use an abacus, but this once revolutionary tool has no place in mathematics going forward. It is, and should remain, a relic.

Even at that young age, the irony of counting buttons with an abacus was not lost on me. If I squinted, the shiny buttons looked just like the beads of the abacus themselves. I'd have to count the buttons, one at a time, and then use the abacus to count them again, moving one bead at a time, more than doubling the amount of work needed to reach the same result since adding up the Hindu-Arabic numerals would have been so much easier.

But Folco was a stubborn man. He wanted his business run *his* way, the only way he knew how.

Not long into my apprenticeship I asked him, "How much does an apprentice normally pay a master?

"100 florins."

But I didn't see that amount anywhere in the daybook.

"I'm sorry. Where's that in the ledger?"

Folco was incredulous. "Why would I put that in the ledger?"

"Since I would have received wages later in my apprenticeship, how will you know when I've worked enough to pay you back?"

Folco grumbled loudly and walked away.

I would like to tell you my relationship with Folco got better from there, but many things I would like to tell you about this world simply aren't true.

I wondered if there was a way to keep track of this type of thing over time. I had heard stories about big merchants in Venice trading goods all over the world. Surely, they had systems to keep track of wages and things like this, making sure that all debts were paid.

Before he died, my godfather had made a name for himself dredging the canals there. I hoped to make a name for myself one day, too. But I was still only twelve, much too young to travel to a city like Venice on my own with no prospects. If only my godfather were still alive, perhaps I could have gone and lived with him, but I was stuck in Folco's shop for the foreseeable future.

2

Chapter Five

THE ALTAR

My eyesight had never been great, but it seemed to deteriorate more and more every day I spent in Folco's shop. After a few years, when I was sixteen, I could hardly see further than its walls. And my prospects seemed limited as well.

I slogged away, but the fabric business wasn't doing, well, much business at all. Customers were few and far between. I wasn't gaining any real experience. And heaven knows, I couldn't count on a recommendation from Folco. I feared no other employer would ever want to hire me.

I thought this might be it. I might work for Folco for the rest of my life, or at least the rest of his. His orneriness seemed to fuel his longevity so that could be a while, but then what? Who would want to hire someone who couldn't see, didn't have a recommendation, and who had only worked in a dusty, decrepit fabric shop in a small town of no consequence?

I tried not to focus on my predicament, but that wasn't always easy. I tended to concentrate on whatever local gossip was circulating through town, whether it be the most recent bout of infidelity or trying to discern which of the priests was breaking his covenant. One day, I heard that the artist Piero della Francesca was unveiling his long-awaited altarpiece for the Chapel of the Misericordia. He had received the commission sixteen years before, about the same time I was born, but he was only just now finishing it.

Everyone in town was abuzz. After all these years the altarpiece was either going to be a masterpiece or a gigantic scandal, if it didn't meet their expectations. I had to attend the unveiling to see which.

It seemed like everyone in town was there or at least a majority, but who's to say? We still hadn't progressed further than the beans when it came to counting ourselves.

I stood at the back of the crowd. When the cloth covering the altarpiece came off I could hear the oohs and ahhs from the gathered horde, but I couldn't see the altarpiece. It was just one big amorphous shape. So I made my way to the front.

Slowly, it came into focus. Although I have since learned the words I could have used to describe how I felt, at the time I had none of them. I stood there, gobsmacked and mesmerized, for what seemed like hours. There was a large Madonna at the center of the altarpiece, her arms wide, spreading her cloak over the gathered worshippers, protecting them as they prayed to her. From where I stood, I felt like she was spreading her cloak over me, protecting me as I bathed in her radiance. The anxiety and worry I felt in Folco's shop melted out of the bottom of my feet.

My eyes grazed the panels, feasting on their sumptuousness. I was particularly moved by five vignettes that lined the bottom of the altarpiece. Unlike the other images in the altarpiece with shimmering gold backdrops, these five had fully realized hills, columns, and trees in the background. Their scenes extended far beyond the main composition, all the way to the horizon and beyond.

It was the first time I had seen anything like it. And judging by the reaction of the crowd, it was the first time they had seen anything like it either. The only people seemingly unimpressed by the altarpiece were a group of young men around my age. They sat casually, chatting and gossiping amongst themselves, seeming to pay no mind to the magnificence that lay only a few feet away from them.

I collected my umbrage in my fists and approached them, determined to see what they found more important than reveling in the altarpiece's majesty.

"What do you think you're doing?"

One of the older boys turned toward me. "Excuse me?"

"You're being disrespectful."

"Who are you? A priest or something?" The other boys started laughing, but that didn't move me from my mission.

"Have you even looked at the altarpiece? It's a great achievement and you're just sitting here. You don't even know what you're missing."

I was sure I had effectively demonstrated how passionate they should be about the altarpiece, but then the older boy made me aware of my folly.

"We're his pupils. We helped make it. So, yeah. We've seen it."

It was like I was standing in front of the altarpiece again. I had no words. Except this time those words were stunted by my mortification and not my amazement. I don't remember what I did or said next, but I wanted to be as far away from there as possible. I wanted to run, but I could feel my chest caving in, restricting my breathing. I'm sure I was gritting my teeth and sweating like the embarrassed mass I was.

But the next thing I remember, I was back in Folco's shop. How did I get there? Surely, I must have walked, but in my shame, I couldn't remember. Part of me hoped the entire incident had been a nightmare that would disappear with the coming day.

But part of me hoped it was a dream. Those boys, ones my age, helped make that altarpiece. They were the pupils of an artist, learning his craft just like I was ostensibly learning Folco's.

I felt like I might go insane with jealousy. What I wouldn't place at that altar to be in their place.

3

Chapter Six

THE RESURRECTION

I wanted to know more. How is it that those boys helped Piero della Francesca with the altarpiece? Did they run errands? Did they fetch water and sweep the floor? Did they simply stand guard over the work when he wasn't there? Surely, they weren't involved in the actual making of it. I'm sure that boy had overstated his bounds.

I needed to find out. I made inquiries about town and discovered that Piero's next project would be a fresco of the Resurrection of Christ in the Communal Palace. I had to see for myself. I stalked my prey to the room where the magistrates and governors met. When I arrived, no one was there. The theory of standing guard was out.

I heard noises and ducked behind a door. I stood in a small triangle of space between door and walls, praying that I wouldn't be found. I peered through the slit and saw a man who must have been Piero, for he was the only adult present, enter the room. His pupils followed closely behind.

Knowing that the altarpiece took him sixteen years, I expected a more languid man to saunter in. But he acted more like a military commander, marching about, barking orders, mustering his pupils and setting them to task. They were collecting tools that I had not seen before. One was a strange device, vaguely in the shape of a capital A with a few knobs and dials protruding. Another was a string with some sort of weight attached to one end.

The pupils handed out pieces of paper and circled around the fresco site. And then Piero did something wholly unexpected. He started lecturing to them. He talked about the fresco and how to execute his plans for it. They seemed to be copying down something that Piero was showing them on the wall, but from my vantage I couldn't see what was going on. I could see the pupils' faces, but not the lesson. I had to find a remedy.

I made my way around the building, all the way around the other entrance to the long room. I peered in through a door at the back. Unfortunately, my eyesight did me no favors. I couldn't see anything. I tried not to be noticed, but Piero's eyesight was obviously much better than mine because he saw me immediately and came at me.

"Hey, you! Boy!"

His outline grew larger as he approached. I could see how annoyed he was as his true image resolved itself on his way over.

"You are to leave at once. I will have no audience. We are busy working."

But I was no mere onlooker. I was a devotee, ready to place myself at his altar, albeit metaphorically this time. He must have noticed the despair on my face because his tone shifted and became more conciliatory. He gestured toward the other side of the room.

"And I don't have time for any new pupils. As you can see, I have enough already."

I couldn't quite make them out, but I had seen them before, so I nodded.

"Even if you were, I wouldn't have any money to give you."

I hung my head and walked away.

Something in the manner I had said this last statement must have resonated with Piero because he soon caught up to me.

"Where do you think you're going?"

"You said . . ."

"What's your name?"

"Luca."

"And what do you do, Luca?"

"I work in Folco de Belfolci's fabric shop."

"Does he treat you well?"

"Well enough," I lied.

"But you're not saving your wages?"

"I will once I start getting them."

"And when is that?"

I shrugged my shoulders. I honestly didn't know. If my family had been able to pay Folco at the beginning of my apprenticeship I would have been receiving wages from him for some time. But since they didn't, I didn't, and I had long given up hope of receiving them anytime in the near future.

Piero sighed. He was mulling something over.

"Well. When you don't have to be at the shop, you can come here."

I didn't know this until years later, but Piero had also been in the unfortunate situation of working as an unpaid apprentice early in his life. Maybe I should have asked more questions about his change in heart, but in that moment, I couldn't have cared less. Mine was exploding with happiness. There were so many questions I wanted to ask about what we were going to be doing, what he would like me to do for him, what his inspiration was, and what his techniques were.

But all I could get out in response was, "Really?"

5

Chapter Seven

PERSPECTIVE

I tried to be at the Communal Palace under Piero's tutelage as much as possible. If you asked Folco about this period in my life he would recall that I was often too ill to work in the shop. I probably played hooky more frequently than I should have.

Piero elucidated the tools I had seen him using. The string with the weight on one end was the plummet line. The capital A with a few knobs on it was the compass. He was a painter, but he considered these tools to be the cornerstone of his practice, not paints and brushes.

"What do you use them for?" I asked, not knowing how a plummet line and compass could even be used in painting.

"Perspective."

Perhaps I shouldn't have been surprised, but Piero would complete a mountain of work before ever picking up a brush. He would toil on the underdrawing, using the plummet line and compass to create a perspective grid, a set of crisscrossing horizontal and vertical lines that mimic the perception of actual depth. Rectangles shift into concave trapezoids to give the illusion of distance. And sometimes those lines would resemble a real mountain.

Like the five vignettes at the bottom of the Madonna altarpiece, this fresco was going to have a realistic background. Christ was going to be in the foreground, with trees and hills extending to the vanishing point.

I was soon able to prove my worth to Piero. The plummet line and compass were only two of the three tools needed to render accurate perspective. The last one was calculation. As soon as he taught me how to do the calculations, I made sure to insert myself in the middle of his work whenever they were needed. He had no trouble doing them himself, but I knew this was an area where I could excel. I wanted my star to shine more brightly than the other pupils so I would perform the calculations quickly, as if my life depended on it. I knew my future did, at least.

This worked well. I was gaining esteem in Piero's eyes, or so I thought. But all this changed when the perspective grid was complete. It was time to move on. Piero moved our attention to the landscape. We grabbed our pieces of paper and encircled the fresco. Piero started drawing the landscape and he told us it was our duty to replicate his sketch. There were no numbers. There were no calculations, other than that between my eye and hand.

I was nervous. I had never really drawn before. Of course, I had done the odd absentminded sketch in my youth, but I had never tried to duplicate something accurately. I closed my hands in prayer hoping that I would have a talent in this area as well.

All the boys rendered their drawings silently. Their eyes squinted, focusing on different details in Piero's sketch and copying them accordingly. I spied on each of their drawings. I could see that every one of them had some small thing wrong with it, but were otherwise all completely admirable reproductions.

All except mine. It was clear on my first day of drawing that I had no natural talent. Drawing straight lines with a plummet line and compass was one thing. Drawing landscapes was another. As I had closed my hands in prayer, I now saw it did not work, and covered my face with my hands instead, fearful that my lack of ability in this area would be my downfall and Piero would send me packing.

Piero frowned when he saw my work. I thought he would give me a scolding. If I were in his position, I would have thought that I hadn't even tried. It looked like I might have done better drawing with my foot. I looked up at him hoping for an encouraging remark.

"That's horrible," he said and then walked out of the room.

This was it. I knew it. He was going to tell me not to come back. He had put up with me long enough. It was clear that there was no reason for me to be here. Any more time spent on me would be wasted.

Piero stuck his head back into the room, "Are you coming or not?"

At least he was doing me the favor of telling me this in the hallway and not in front of the others, I thought.

I tried to join him in the hallway, but as soon as I reached it, Piero was already on his way down the stairs.

"Let's go."

He was walking fast, almost jogging. Piero kept up this quick pace as I trailed him down the street.

"Keep up!"

I tried to, but he was possessed. I was never able to fully catch up and walk at his side, and remained a few paces behind.

We walked all the way up the hill to the monastery. As soon as we crested the hill, Piero launched into a speech.

"There are many ways to draw a landscape. To do it justice, though, you cannot merely try and copy down what you see. You have to learn how to view it correctly. That's what I'm teaching you with the perspective grid. And it is something that you can learn. I had a steep learning curve and it's blatantly clear that you will too." Piero smiled a bit. "The first horse I ever drew, I was so proud of it. I showed it to my father and he complimented me . . . on having drawn a rather lovely bush. But I was able to get the hang of it."

What was he saying? Was he going to let me stay? It seemed like he was encouraging me, but I wasn't sure. Outside of the friars at school, I wasn't used to the feeling. I wanted to stop him and confirm that I was hearing him correctly, but he kept lecturing.

"I learned perspective from Leon Battista Alberti in his book *Della Pittura* at the duke's library at Urbino. Alberti isn't much of a painter, but his book contains an analysis of all the painting techniques and theories yet known. All except a few I've developed. But I'm getting ahead of myself. Tell me, when you look at this landscape. What do you see?"

From where we were standing we could see the entire town and surrounding forest, or at least that's what I knew I was supposed to see, but couldn't. I couldn't tell much of a difference between the blue sky and what lay below. I could make out the shape of the horizon, but not much more.

"I can't."

"I'm willing to give you a shot, but you have to try," Piero said, mistaking my inability for a lack of ambition.

"No, I can't. I can't see that far. As long as I can remember . . . other people describe things far away and I just . . . I can't see them."

If I was previously unsure of how the day would end, Piero's response to my confession confirmed my worst fears, or so I thought.

"You can calculate the vanishing point, but can't see one? This won't do. I can't teach someone who can't see."

8

Chapter Eight

SIGHT

"You're a myope," the shop man said.

I hadn't heard this slur before, but I was sure it was something city people called us country folk. Piero had taken me forty miles over the Apennine Mountains to Urbino. It was just a mid-sized city, but to me, it could have just as easily been Venice or Florence. It was the big city compared to my small town of Sansepulcro.

But the shop man wasn't being mean. He was trying to help me. He had me sit down on a chair in his shop. Piero told him I had trouble seeing the horizon and he explained that a myope was someone who couldn't see things far away. It wasn't a denigration. It was a description. And it was his job to help those that fit it.

The man kept putting these odd little contraptions on my face. He called them *occhiale*, glasses for the eyes.

"Can you see?" he would ask after placing them on my nose.

I shook my head, my shame welling up inside me. He tried

out pair after pair, but they only made my eyesight worse. He seemed to have so many different kinds of eyeglasses, but none of them were working.

None of them fixed me. I was irrevocably broken and I always would be. I could feel an odd pulling at the back of my collar, and could have sworn it was death himself coming to get me early, knowing I would amount to nothing, giving him the opportunity to reap my soul before its natural end.

But the feeling I felt on the back of my neck was nothing other than a bit of string hanging off the shop man's pants. He stood on a stool near me and grabbed a small box off a high shelf.

He glided a new pair on my face and all of a sudden . . . *BAM!* I could see out the window and all the way down the street!

I leaped from the chair and ran out of the shop. I had to make sure I was actually looking at a real street and not a painting of one. I had to know it was real and that I could touch it, smell it . . . see it. And I could.

It's hard to describe to people who don't need eyeglasses how freeing this moment was. In a way, it felt like I had just been born. The world was somehow brighter. And it was big, so much bigger. I don't know how, but I could feel its size expanding. It was like there was this new enormity that I was able to tap into.

I don't think I'd ever smiled as much as I did that day, or since. But even as happy as I was, reality set in. I was sure I couldn't afford anything like this. Why did Piero bring me here? Was it to torture me after wasting his time? I walked meekly back into the shop, a complete reversal of my jubilant exit.

"How much do these cost?"

The man went over to a shelf with a wide variety of eyeglasses.

"Well. There are a few options. There are these ordinary,

run-of-the-mill ones that are two or three. There are these ones, much better quality, six to eighteen soldi. And then, there are these. They have the absolute finest crystal lenses. And the frame is silver. Aren't they exquisite?"

I don't have to tell you, but they were.

"And how much are they?" Piero asked.

"Only one ducat."

A whole ducat. I don't think my family ever had a whole ducat at one time. To my surprise, the ordinary ones were reasonably priced. I could have easily afforded them if I had been earning wages from Folco.

"We'll take it, the crystal and silver ones," Piero said.

"No, no!" I said. "I can't even afford the . . ."

"I'm paying for them. Obviously," Piero chided, cutting me off.

"The run-of-the-mill ones will be fine."

"If I wanted a run-of-the-mill pupil, I would get you run-of-the-mill glasses."

The day before, I had been sure that Piero was going to get rid of me. And now he was buying eyeglasses for me that cost a whole ducat. I felt so lucky. Not only for his kindness, but to be alive right now. The lenses in my new extraordinarily beautiful glasses, the ones that help me and others see far distances, had only been invented in Florence shortly before I was born and now they had reached Urbino. If I had been born twenty years earlier, I might not have been able to savor their greatness. That day was one of the first times I realized how amazing the world is, and how rapidly Italy was changing.

I promised myself that I would pay Piero back. It would probably take me a long time to do it, but I would raise the ducat and return it to him.

I looked forward to that day, but I knew even when it came it would never be enough. I could never fully repay Piero for those glasses and the feeling they gave me. And for that I am eternally grateful.

13

Chapter Nine

THE LIBRARY

"Do you want to meet the Duke of Urbino?" Piero asked. "I have to deliver a painting."

I did. But there was something else I wanted to do more.

"Can I go to the library instead? I want to read that book on perspective you told me about."

I instantly felt bad. Piero had just bought me the most beautiful pair of glasses. It was the kindest thing anyone had done for me. I was his pupil and instead of helping him deliver a painting I wanted to ditch him and read a book, something I could do without my new glasses.

I thought he might be upset, but he smiled. I had seen him smile before, but there was something different about this one. His eyes more wistful, and maybe, was there a bit of mist in them as well?

"Of course," Piero said.

The duke's library was private so Piero had to introduce me to the librarian.

"He's with me," Piero told him.

I shouldn't have been surprised, but the two men seemed like old friends. I think they started catching up with one another, but my attention was drawn elsewhere.

There were hundreds and hundreds of books, more than I had ever seen in one place. It may sound silly to you, but there were more books in that library than I thought existed in the entire world. And the library itself was gorgeous. On the ceiling, there was a painting of a resplendent eagle enveloped in flames. Fire shot out in all directions and lit up the books on the rich, dark wood shelves that lined the walls.

"We'll dine with the duke at seven," Piero said.

He pointed at a clock in the library, one of the first I'd seen.

"Don't be late. He hates it if you're late," Piero said as he left.

Given that information, I didn't want to waste any time.

"Do you have Leon Batista Alberti's *Della Pittura*?" I asked the librarian.

He nodded toward an older man on a table at the far side of the library. I could see the top of his head behind a stack of books he'd laid out in front of him. I'd been so impressed by the library that I hadn't noticed the man.

"He's reading it," the librarian said.

The man seemed to be about sixty years old. And busy. His focus was so intense that I dared not disturb him. So, I waited. It was a few hours before dinner. There was plenty of time so I decided to peruse some other books while I waited.

It was in this library at Urbino that I first experienced hunger. Yes, I had felt pangs of hunger when I needed to eat, but this was new. There were rows upon rows of books. I wasn't desperate for dinner. Rather, I wanted to consume every tome I could find.

It was glorious. I skimmed book after book, making mental notes to return and devour them thoroughly at a future date. But none were the volume that I came for. The old man was still monopolizing that one.

I had been patient, but now I could see that there was only a half hour until dinner. If I didn't act fast I wouldn't be able to glean any knowledge from the book. I needed to learn the secrets of perspective. I needed to start repaying my debt to Piero. I didn't know when I'd be able to come back so this might be my only chance.

I marched right up to the old man.

"There are other people who want to read this book, you know!"

"That's always good to hear," he said.

"So, are you done?"

"Well, if I haven't learned all I can from it by now, I don't know what hope I have."

His response led me to believe that he would hand it over, but he made no such effort. He just kept looking at me, peering at me with an intense gaze. I remember thinking that I hadn't really seen his face until now. It had been buried in the book. The man had a big, protruding nose that provided an ample platform for his glasses.

"Can I have it?" I interrogated.

"I have a puzzle for you. If you can solve it, I'll teach you everything you'd ever want to know about this book."

"I don't have time for games. I have dinner with the duke at seven."

"Oh, you do. Very nice."

I could tell he was patronizing me. "What can you teach me?" I asked impertinently.

"First things first," he said, and slid me a piece of paper. "Tell me what this says."

It read:

BFYBGVZXOBKBLORFOQDKLNANAXZEEXOCSYLX HLSEEXRB&RBSIFVREACDAO.

This old man was trying to bewilder me, but right away, I knew what it was. Or rather, I knew how to solve it. I'd show him. I'd seen ciphers before. We would pass around notes using ciphers in school. Caesar invented them to keep his private correspondence private and we used them to keep our messages from being decoded by our teachers. I don't remember actually communicating anything important enough or disparaging enough to merit the secrecy, but it was one of our favorite pastimes nonetheless.

Ciphers substitute one letter for another. Since some letters occur more often than others, I needed to analyze the frequency of the letters in the cipher to determine the original text. The vowels E, A, I, and O are the most common characters in Italian and this cipher had a lot of Bs, a good number of Os, and some As and Xs too. So, these letters were the most likely candidates for my vowels. I knew that if I could figure out a small part of the message, I would have the key to decode the rest. If I found out that an A should be an E, then I would know that an L should be a P, and so forth, and that every letter in the cipher should be shifted five places in the alphabet.

The wheels were turning in my head. I was trying to form small words with the cipher, using the common ones like "the," "for," "with," and "and" that would unlock the meaning of the rest. But nothing was lining up. None of the small words were working. Then I tried a few bigger ones like "book," "library," and "perspective" to no avail. There weren't *any* words present in the cipher as far as I could tell. In addition, there was that ampersand. I'd never seen one in a cipher before. I thought it was benign. It was probably just an ampersand, not part of the cipher itself. How could it be a part of the cipher? It's not part of the alphabet!

Then it hit me. There was something more complex going on here than I'd ever encountered before. Or else it was just gibberish. In that moment, I concluded it was the latter.

"This is nonsense."

"It is?"

"Yeah, there's no message here. It's just random letters."

"And how do you know that?"

"Because frequency analysis doesn't work."

"You're right, frequency analysis doesn't work on it, but it's not nonsense."

Then he placed a small wooden wheel on the table. It had two concentric rings of letters on it, but there were some differences between the two. The outer ring was uppercase and the inner one was lowercase. And it wasn't just letters. The ampersand was on the inside ring and the numbers 1, 2, 3 and 4 were on the outside.

I noticed that since the letters on the inside of the ring weren't alphabetical, the technique I was using wouldn't have worked. But it was still solvable.

"It's still a substitution cipher. You just need this wooden . . ."

"Formula," he interjected.

"To solve it," I finished.

"Maybe . . ." he said, trailing off a bit in the way that one does in order to build suspense.

"Maybe what?" I asked impertinently, cutting his drama a bit short, not being the proper audience member I should have been.

"But what if you were encoding the message and you changed the position after every letter?"

He moved the inner ring. I hadn't noticed that the two were connected via a pin in the middle.

I finally started to get it. "So, you'd need the Formula, the starting point, and how many places forward you skip after each letter," I said, my mind was racing with possibilities, possibilities that I couldn't contain to myself.

"That is, that is," I stammered, "if you keep it a consistent amount. Changing up the number of places you skip forward could be an added variable too," I concluded, although it really was more of a question.

"That's perspective," he said.

What was he talking about? The book he was keeping from me was about perspective. Not this.

He could see the puzzled look on my face.

"There are many types of perspective. There's the visual kind in this book. The mental one you just demonstrated. The ability to see beyond what's in front of you. When I invented the Formula, it took my colleagues days to figure out that normal frequency analysis wouldn't work."

Wait. This old man invented this? I was flabbergasted. The Formula was truly revolutionary and here I was talking with him.

"How did you come up with something like this?"

"Same as when I wrote this book. First there was Brunelleschi. Then there was *Witelo's Perspectiva*, a book on optics based on the work of Ibn al-Haytham. He was an Arab mathematician. That was a fun translation. So, you see, I built my work on the backs of others."

I understood the optics and Arab mathematician bit. But the first thing he said really confused me. He was referring to the book in front of him. The book I wanted to read. The book that Piero said taught him perspective. It couldn't be.

"That means you're . . . ?"

"Yes, I'm Leon Battista Alberti."

21

Chapter Ten

THE COURT OF EARTHLY DELIGHTS

I was so embarrassed. I tried to apologize to Alberti, but he looked past my shoulder and swatted away my attempt.

"We're late," he said tersely and shut his book.

I spun around to see the clock taunting me, telling me I was a disappointment. It was ten minutes past seven. Being on time was the one thing Piero told me to do and I couldn't even do that. Should I even go? I could fake an injury of some kind. My chest already felt like it was caving in, perhaps I could say that one of my lungs fell out. That would give me the alibi I needed.

Alberti interrupted my panic. "Come on," he said from the doorway.

Together, we rushed down hallway after hallway. There were so many of them. Was this all the same building? We were hoofing it at a brisk pace, but Alberti slowed down markedly as we approached the entrance to the large dining hall where the duke ate his meals. I was right behind him and almost slammed into him when his gait stagnated.

Alberti entered calmly as if he hadn't just been running at a brisk pace. I tried to follow suit.

"You're late," the duke bellowed as we breached the hall.

"Am I? The clock in the library said I would be early," Alberti lied.

"No, no," the duke said and pointed to a large, fancy wooden clock, the grand centerpiece of the room.

"All the clocks in Urbino, especially the ones in the palace, are set off this clock. Daily life in the city is measured accurately and consistently."

"Really?" I asked, perhaps a bit too loudly. No one seemed to notice my presence before, but now all eyes were on me.

"Of course!" the duke said, a bit flustered. "Who are you?"

To my surprise, Piero and Alberti answered simultaneously. "He's with me."

"Very well then," the duke nodded. Servants emerged with gleaming silver trays filled to the brim with venison, pheasant, rabbit, and mutton. I hadn't eaten much meat before, an occasional chicken or ham being the extent of my experience with animal flesh, salt prices being what they were.

There were delicacies of all sorts. There was *polenta e osei*. But nothing could prepare me for what they brought out next. Standing stiff and careful, so as not to spill, two servers emerged carrying a swan and peacock, or at least the remains of those majestic birds. The peacock was the more resplendent of the two, the ducal cooks having reattached the feathers of the peacock for decoration. The rainbow plumage of the male peacock fanned out in all directions, enticing us to savor its meat just as the peacock had once tried to entice its mate.

I wondered if these were the feathers of the same bird that was now to be our dinner, or if they merely employed the same set of feathers for each and every occasion. The more I thought about it, though, the more I hoped that these feathers were merely plucked, and this magnificent male peacock only had to shed its feathers and not its mortal coil.

As I was accustomed to eating mush or soup, or sometimes mushy soup, for each and every meal, the sumptuousness of this supper was not lost on me. The bread here was not black, but a crisp golden brown. Just the smell sent my taste buds soaring.

I was used to eating a hodgepodge of whatever I could find, scrapped vegetables and nearly rotten eggs, and stewing them in a cauldron. As I stirred, I remember praying that the cauldron's contents would magically transform into an edible meal. But it was only now that I felt my prayers had finally been answered.

For a moment I thought Alberti was savoring the succulent smells of these delectable dishes as much as I was, wafting the meaty air toward his nostrils, but it turned out he was beckoning me to our seats. Having been lost in wonderment, I apparently needed a guide to navigate this new terrain.

I tracked Alberti over to our seats near Piero.

As soon as we sat down, Alberti asked, "Federico, I was wondering if you might extend the use of your library to this young man. It's been made clear to me that no one should stand between this lad and his books."

Federico da Montefeltro was, of course, the duke's Christian name. They must have been on familiar terms for him to use it. I couldn't imagine why Alberti was using his relationship with the duke to get me ongoing access to the library, but I was pleased nonetheless.

Alberti continued. "You see, he wanted to read my *Della Pittura*, but since I was currently occupied with it . . ."

"You were reading your own book?" Piero asked incredulously.

"Of course."

"Why on earth would you do that?"

"To see if the text still stands up."

"I don't stare at my paintings, gazing up at them in admiration. I let others do that for me."

Alberti turned to the duke. "Are you going to hear cases tonight or am I the one on trial?"

I was confused. I would learn later that the duke regularly decided legal cases when he was at dinner, dispensing justice between bites. But that's not what confused me. I thought that Piero and Alberti would have been friendly, but they were at each other's throats.

"No, not tonight," the duke answered. "Tonight we get to celebrate the unveiling of a new work by Signore Piero della Francesca himself. His . . . what are you calling it?"

"*The Flagellation of Christ*," Piero stated.

"How lovely," the duke replied coyly.

Then two servants pulled a sheet off an easel to reveal the painting. Immediately, those around me started oohing and aahing just like the crowd at the unveiling of Piero's altarpiece.

The painting featured two groups of men, one in the foreground and the other in the back. That was the group that was whipping Christ. With my new glasses, I could see how well Piero had used perspective in the painting.

"Very nice," Alberti proclaimed. "But you should accompany this young man to the library and visit my book yourself. If you did, you would know that the vanishing point should be at the eye level of the subject."

"Oh, I've read it," Piero responded. "You can't do that for every painting though. It limits your compositions. Makes them rather stale, don't you think? You see, I've taken your techniques and built upon them, finding more practical applications for painters. I'm sure if you had any real talent as a painter you would understand."

With that, the room fell silent. There was no room for sound with the deafening tension that descended upon us. I don't know why, but I thought it appropriate for me to say something.

"Don't worry, I'm not good at painting either."

Then, all of a sudden, everyone burst out laughing. Everyone except me, that is. What did I say that was so funny?

Although I hadn't said this last question out loud, the duke seemed to field my query. "In lieu of any courtly dramatics this evening, you two have admirably stepped up to fill the void."

I saw Piero and Alberti smile at one another and then get back to their meals.

That's when it clicked. They were just play fighting. Luckily, the fruit course had arrived so the attention of the room shifted to the fruits and nuts and cheeses and jellies the servers brought in. To this day, I should like to remember all that they brought in for dessert that evening, or rather, the fruit course, even though they served much more than fruit. I would like to have such a better recollection of that, my first courtly dinner, but my mind was still reeling from what I thought was surely the most horrible faux pas ever committed, not yet realizing that the room had quickly moved on.

"I will miss you dearly. Are you sure you have to leave for Venice?" the duke asked.

"Unfortunately, yes," said Alberti.

Venice? He was going to Venice? As you know, I had long dreamed of going there. I was immensely jealous of Alberti even though he had probably gone many times before and this instance would be of no consequence.

I figured I couldn't embarrass myself any more than I already had, so I launched a series of questions at him. In my excitement, I didn't even give him the courtesy of a short pause between inquiries. Rather, I let them spew out in a torrent like rain out of a gutter in a storm.

"Is it true that it's a city built on the ocean? Do the merchants really accept cheques from China and Baghdad? Are books being printed there now?" I inquired breathlessly.

"Well, why don't you see for yourself? If you like, I'll find a job for you there. Would you like that?"

Was that a real question? My answer spurted out of my mouth.

"Of course I would!"

34

Chapter Eleven

THE WAIT

Alberti promised to write when he found a job for me. But after a few months I started to lose confidence that he would.

Did he forget about me? That was entirely possible. The next day after he left the palace I had to chase down his horse cart when I realized he didn't know my name or where to send the letter. And I was so out of breath when I caught up with him that I forgot to ask for the solution to the cipher he had given me.

But I didn't spend too much time worrying. I spent as many hours as I could in the duke's library. I dove into the books I had promised to return to, and then some. In one, Plato wrote, "Tell me where you've been and I'll tell you what you know." As a small-town boy who hadn't been anywhere in his life, this was humbling, but at the same time I felt like I could travel anywhere in the world in these books. It was incredibly liberating.

Although I had only just started as Piero's pupil, he

frequently gave me leave to attend to my studies in the library. Unfortunately, my new glasses didn't help me become better at drawing. Despite my best efforts, my skill did not improve in drawing landscapes. Or people. Or animals. Or buildings. Or anything really that didn't involve a straight line and mathematical calculation.

I was nervous that Alberti would find a job for me working with another artist since I was technically, if not effectively, an artist's pupil. So, Piero did me the favor of writing Alberti a letter, suggesting that the job for me should involve mathematics since I was strong in that area.

A year passed by. I kept assisting Piero as best I could. He finished his Resurrection of Christ fresco and was set to move onto something else. At the same time, I was still ostensibly, believe it or not, working in Folco's shop and still living with him. My rope with him grew shorter and shorter every day. I skipped work so often that he broke down and threatened to kick me out if I missed one more day in his shop.

At the time, this scared me, but there was no sweating, no chest caving. I no longer had to be afraid of the possible repercussions. I knew he would do it. And I was numb. I didn't know what I would do if Folco kicked me out. I didn't know where I would go. All I knew was that after he gave me that ultimatum, I had to go to the library. I had given up hope that Alberti would find me a job, but it was the one place where I felt confident and in control of my destiny.

I left Sansepulcro that day knowing full well that there would be no place for me upon my return. I knew the library had a new tome on the history of Thebes. So at least I knew I could go to Thebes, if only in my mind's eye. When I arrived to the library that day, the librarian greeted me soundlessly, nodding politely as he normally would, and then slid an envelope across his desk. I looked at him in shock.

"What is this?" I implored.

"It looks like a letter. Why don't you open it and find out?"

I opened it, my hands trembling.

The letter began:

Dear Luca,

I sent this letter to you at the duke's library knowing that if you received it here you would still be the man I put up for the position . . .

55

Chapter Twelve

O SEA

The next thing I knew I was standing in front of Ser Antonio de Rompiasi's house.

He answered the door and said, "Good, you're here. Let's go," before I could even glance at him. He led me through his shop, all the way to the canal on the other side. A small boat was waiting for us.

"Get in. I've got a surprise for you."

I got a better look at him as we sailed through the canal. His face had a stern expression to it, but there was kindness in it as well. I hoped his disposition would be the latter. I prayed to God that he wouldn't be another Folco. I tried to discern which one it would be, but the waves were getting larger and it was hard to focus on his face.

Then everything started spinning. I had never been on water this choppy before and I soon demonstrated my naiveté by getting sick over the side of the boat.

A flotilla of merchant boats awaited us at the entrance of

the Adriatic. Soon a man in a small boat like Rompiasi's sailed up. It was odd. He was wearing full wedding regalia, including a light blue waistcoat, but there was no bride in a light blue dress to match.

All the boats parted for him and he glided right into the middle of the flotilla. He was, as I would learn, the doge, the ruler of Venice.

He made two loud coughing sounds and then began his grand pronouncement, "O sea, we wed thee in a sign of our true and everlasting dominion."

Then, and this part still tickles me, he tossed a diamond ring into the water! He married the sea!

A few men jumped in trying to retrieve the ring, but none came up a bride, although some of them did look blue in the face.

Rompiasi turned to me and smiled.

"Welcome to Venice."

89

Chapter Thirteen

THE MERCHANT OF VENICE

R ompiasi lived in the Guidecca, a small island district in the southern part of the city. Once a home to the banished and the Jews, it was now a district in demand. All the best families wanted to live there and Rompiasi did.

My job was to tutor his two sons. Additionally, I would help him in his business affairs. Like many Venetian merchants, he ran his shop out of the ground, or sea level, floor of his house. The walls were covered with marine charts. He was an alum trader, a part of a Medici-controlled network distributing alum from a recently discovered mine near Rome. It was the first alum mine discovered outside Constantinople, a major development for the fabric industry. Having worked in Folco's dilapidated shop, I knew how much Rompiasi's trade would help save small merchants like Folco. I was happy for Folco even though I was elated to escape his purview. His business would improve, although it might not help much with his disposition.

Rompiasi showed me how he kept his books. He had a

daybook ledger like Folco, but he had another book with two columns running down every page. It was much more complicated than Folco's system, and I became overwhelmed. I'm sure my eyes glazed over. Suddenly, it felt like the eyeglasses Piero had purchased for me were no longer worth the silver they were made out of. I felt lightheaded and brought a shaky hand up to my forehead.

"Is there a manual for this method? What's it called?" I asked.

"The Venetian method, I suppose. There's no manual. Every merchant has his own way of doing it. Some even keep two copies of their books, if you know what I mean."

I didn't exactly know what he meant, but it sounded duplicitous.

"And even if there was a manual, most of them wouldn't use it anyway. It's hard to teach an old dog new tricks."

Having worked with Folco, I knew this was true.

"Folco had me fill in the daybook, but there wasn't a second step."

Rompiasi settled in to explain. "The main thing you need to know is that everything gets counted twice, once in each column. There's a debit side and a credit side. That way, at the end of the day, you can see . . ."

"If everything adds up," I interrupted. I could feel the blood rushing back to my head although with a renewed sense of confidence. "It makes it easy to check your work."

"Precisely," Rompiasi responded.

I could get the hang of this.

144

Chapter Fourteen

A NEW LANGUAGE

Plato was right. There was so much I would have never known if I had not come to Venice. I could have read that it's a city built on top of the sea, a marvel of engineering. I could have read that there are clogged mud banks and half-drowned fields next to grand, opulent buildings. I could have read that even though the city was still a work in progress, only Paris and Naples were bigger. But I couldn't have read about the energy. Venice was a city on the brink of the future, a gleaming example of possibility.

The feeling of wonder I got in the Duke of Urbino's library was now multiplied. Incense, perfumes, and spices filled my nostrils, masking the stink of the canals. People from all over the world were coming to Venice to trade goods, ideas, and culture. Their languages filled my ears. In addition to Veneto, which I had to get used to, there was Yiddish and Ladino, German, French, and Spanish. There was Turkish, Slav, and Arabic. I heard so many languages spoken, I felt as if I could travel the world just by traversing the city's narrow canals.

The most exciting language spoken in Venice, though, was mathematics. And I wanted to be fluent. I continued my studies at the Scuola di Rialto with Bragadino, the eminent public lecturer. There was no textbook, so I wrote down everything he said. I didn't want to miss a word. He was a natural lecturer, bringing together the teachings of the ancient Greek and Arab mathematicians in a way that seemed to fit our multitudinous and cacophonous city. In a sea of languages, mathematics pierced through them all, calling me with its siren song. In a city of possibility, mathematics held the most promise. It was the one field that could push forward all others along with it.

I wanted to convey this to the Rompiasi boys as their tutor, but I didn't know where to start. Similar to my own studies, there was no textbook from which to teach them. I figured since Plato was right about travel, he had to be right about teaching as well. It is said that he wrote, "Let no one ignorant of geometry enter," above the door to his academy. So, I decided to begin with geometry, but soon learned that I was no Bragadino.

I sat there, staring forward, palms sweaty, nervous to begin my first lesson. But I couldn't begin. I had a churning in my stomach whose waves seemed to match that of the most tempestuous sea, so I decided, very suddenly, to visit the nearest canal and bestow upon it the contents of my breakfast.

Unfortunately, but perhaps fittingly for boys of their age and disposition, this was the highlight of my first lesson for the Rompiasi boys. They laughed and chortled their way through the rest of the day, and any time they would see me henceforth.

My lessons were tortured. The boys tried to write down my words, but I struggled to string sentences together, let alone connect the concepts in their minds. In the wake of my personal failing, I decided to start writing my lessons down. It helped me save face and a few breakfasts, but it also helped the boys learn. Their progress was precipitous as long as my lessons were on the page.

One day after a particularly good lecture from Bragadino, in which I marveled at both the material and his innate sense of delivery, I met the man who would be my principal companion in Venice. His name was Antonio Cornaro, the second amiable Antonio in my Venetian adventure. Like myself, he was a student devoted to paying rapturous attention to Bragadino and bathing in the promise of mathematics. Quite unlike myself, though, he was born into one of the twelve families of nobility in Venice. And we were neighbors—yet he lived in one of the biggest houses in the Giudecca.

Through this friendship I discovered many of the more diverting entertainments in the city. We would go to see the choir of San Marco. We would dine out in the nicest restaurants. Antonio didn't seemed to mind, but I hated that I could never fully pay my share. I'd hand over what I could and Antonio would cover the deficit. I had a nice wage from Rompiasi, but it wasn't enough to cover lavish feasts in the city's fanciest establishments.

And we would go out dancing. I particularly liked the ones where Antonio and I, along with the other men, sat in a circle. The band would play and the women would walk around and pluck us from our seats for the duration of the evening.

Ah, to be young in Venice again. If the young friar transcribing this book had not already committed himself to the Brotherhood, I would suggest he make a pilgrimage there. My daily routine alternated between helping Rompiasi with his shop, tutoring his sons, soaking up Bragadino's lectures, and exploring the avenues of fine Venetian living with Antonio.

I spent the next six years of my life in this manner. I was on top of the world, or so I thought, living the life I dreamed of as a boy in Sansepulcro. I never wanted it to end, but then one day, it all did.

Rompiasi died.

233

Chapter Fifteen

THE CIPHER

I was twenty-four and had no patron or prospects. I needed to figure out what I would do, but what would that be? I had no idea. My coffers were low. Nights spent savoring the city had depleted my savings even though I was not bearing its full cost. Antonio offered me work with his family, but I couldn't accept his charity. He had been such a good friend to me already. I didn't want to enter a situation where that friendship might be put in peril. Workmates often have to choose which angle of their relationship is the most acute.

I briefly thought about taking the guides I made for the Rompiasi boys to a book publisher. For their studies, I'd written manuals on geometry, algebra, and the Venetian double-entry bookkeeping method and I thought other students might benefit from my summations. The first printing presses in Venice had just opened. While it cost three times as much to set up and print a book as to have a scribe duplicate the same work, you could print 1,000 copies on a printing press with the same amount a scribe would charge to make one manuscript; a marvelous advance in efficiency.

But I didn't want to get ahead of myself. I planned to go to a few booksellers in town before I approached a printer in order to make sure my wares had a market. I soon discovered, though, that they were only selling the Bible and other ecclesiastical texts. It seemed fitting that they would focus on disseminating His word, but I was dismayed. Perhaps these were just the tomes they were selling to the public? Surely, they were printing academic works as well, but were selling them straight to universities. I went to the university library and saw the fate of my manuals sealed on the shelf. I came across a manuscript, not a copy from a printer but a manuscript, from none other than Leon Battista Alberti himself. It was his new treatise on cryptography *De componendis Cifris* (*On devising Ciphers*), using the Formula and polyalphabetic substitution system he had shown me in Urbino. Alberti had written it for Vatican use, but apparently Bragadino had been able to secure a copy for the university library. I was gobsmacked. If Alberti's breakthrough wasn't published on the presses, even though its initial run would have been limited, then my manuals stood no chance!

I remembered how embarrassed I was all those years ago when I found out that that old man monopolizing the book I wanted to read was its author. I smiled. It's funny how perceptions shift over time. What was once a horrible memory is now a happy one.

In this moment of reminiscence, I recalled that I still had the slip of paper Alberti gave me, the one with the cipher. I rushed back to the Rompiasi house to retrieve it before quickly returning to the university library. Now, after all these years, here in front of me was the code to cracking it.

I didn't have a wooden Formula in front of me, but I had the next best thing, a full written description of how it works. So, I made my own Formula out of paper, making the two circles of the Formula with a compass, glad to have it leading me in the right direction.

Now I just needed to figure out the starting point and how many places it skipped forward after each letter. Fortunately, it wasn't hard to figure out. Alberti had taken it easy on me, relatively speaking. He'd left it more or less on the default setting.

It only took me a few minutes to decode the string. Then I needed to break it up into words. I added in a couple Hs where he apparently deemed them unimportant.

This gave me:

What I have learned without pretense I share with others without jealousy.

You may notice, it's a holy dictum. A religious aphorism. I sent Alberti a letter with the deciphered phrase and an update on my circumstances. I prayed he would remember our encounter as fondly as I did. But he was an important man. He was working for the pope now. Any memory of me had surely faded.

As before, I spent my days searching for solace in the library, but I didn't have to wait long for his response this time, because it came quickly. I felt like I held his letter longer in my hand than it took to receive it. I was nervous. The last letter Alberti sent me changed my life.

Would this one?

377

Chapter Sixteen

WHEN IN ROME

If Venice was a city on the rise, then Rome was markedly one on the decline. The outer suburbs had returned to nature. People openly pillaged Rome's Colosseum. It was a city of ruins, but in one important way Rome was still the center of the world—the Church.

I didn't know whether my new job would be ruinous as well, but I was happy to have it. Alberti asked me to be his assistant. He was working for the Church designing aqueducts, naves, and anything that the Church wanted him to work on, or at least that's what he said in his letter.

I was scared. Rome was still a new city and I had never worked in architecture before. I thought the subject might be over my head so I studied as much as I could before my arrival. The stakes of my job in Rome would be much higher. If I messed up an alum shipment I would be out of Rompiasi's favor, but if I made a mistake in my new position I might have the wrath of God reign down upon me.

Alberti greeted me warmly, though, and quickly put my mind at ease. My job would mainly involve fetching books for him in the Vatican Library. He had trouble going to the library himself and it was my duty to rectify the situation. He was even more the old man of my memory.

Alberti acted like an elder statesman. He spent his days using the keys he'd developed over many years, the keys to unlock and access various types of knowledge. He consulted on projects, but rarely carried them out himself. He still had use of an assistant, though, or was at least capable of putting one on the payroll.

I didn't think a job like this was possible. I had imagined it in my dreams, but never expected it to become a reality. I spent my days wandering the aisles of the Vatican Library, the most glorious manifestation of knowledge in Christendom and all the world. And here I was working for the man that built it. Yes, you might read that Pope Nicholas V built it, but that was with Alberti's guidance. It housed the largest collection of manuscripts in Europe, including the ones that I was the most interested in, the work of ancient Greek and Arabic mathematicians.

Manuscripts were flooding in. Many parts of Constantinople were sacked and disseminated after its fall. In my mind, these manuscripts were the city's most precious loot. For many of these books, this was their first visit to Italy and as one of the few people who had access to them, I wanted to give them a warm welcome.

Alberti arranged for me to stay with him at St. Pietro in Vincoli, a short distance north of the Colosseum. Cardinal Francesco della Rovere oversaw this church and I became friends with his nephew Guiliano, who was already sporting the beard he would become known for. He lived at St. Pietro in Vincoli too, and was only a few years older than I was. He had studied the sciences in Perugia.

We hit it off. Guiliano became the Antonio Cornaro of my time in Rome, the companion who opened up the possibilities of the city. If Venice was a young vivacious woman, then Rome was her mother, dressed in black, on her way to church. But this old girl still had some life in her.

One particular morning, I groggily went to see who was persistently knocking on my door. It was Guiliano. I was surprised that he was up early, given the particularly successful evening we had together, but what he told me would have awakened the devil himself, and probably did.

"The pope is dead!"

Those four words, four simple words, set off a chain reaction in the city.

Dong! Dong! Dong! I could hear the bell ring out as surely as if it were in the room next to me, but I knew it wasn't. This was no ordinary bell.

"Is it from the Capitoline?" I asked.

Guiliano nodded.

I had only heard the dull, gloomy tone of the Patara, the name of the Capitoline bell, to bookend Carnival. This time, though, it portended a period much more ominous in the minds of Romans. The period where the seat was empty. *Sede Vacante.*

As soon as they heard the bell, *rione* from each district would distribute the knowledge of the pope's passing to every household, should they somehow have missed the chime of the bell that every Roman's ear had been tuned to since birth. They would go door-to-door, knocking and shouting to fellow citizens that they should place candles in their windows, in order to bring back some light to the city that had just lost a major source of light and inspiration.

Often though, the citizens of Rome were too busy boarding up their windows to place candles in them. For what should have been purely a period of mourning often turned into one of rage, but not rage at the pope's passing. With the seat vacant, Romans took the opportunity to demonstrate their fury at any slight they felt had been done to them, both by the Church and their neighbors.

An orgy of violence swept across the city almost as fast as the intonations of the Patara. No one was safe. Even priests could be attacked, and especially those that had been close to the pope. Fire seemed to engulf a building on every block. The statues of our ancestors, both ancient and new, were torn down.

Mobs roamed the city. One of priests even slashed his way through proponents of the late pontiff, arguing that offices at the Lateran should only be granted to Romans, an obvious condemnation of our other Italian brothers, but in particular the Venetian.

Why? What was the cause of all this hatred? Why all this killing, looting, and burning? What was it all for? A younger version of myself would have asked, "Why are they throwing stones?" I would have asked these questions of my fellow Roman citizens, but in *Sede Vacante* my throat seemed permanently closed, causing me to swallow hard with every breath. I could hardly look into any man's eyes, afraid of seeing complicity in the activities surrounding us. Afraid of what he had done, or was about to do.

I prayed. I prayed and I prayed on these questions. Hard. And then I realized, the seat was never truly vacant. For when the pope passes, the devil takes his place until a new pope rises to take the throne back from him. That was the only way to explain this failure of humanity, this need deep down for Romans to purge themselves of their less-than-heavenly inclinations.

Only the election of a new pope could quell the devil's bloodlust.

610

Chapter Seventeen

THE CONCLAVE

Guiliano and I joined the throngs in St. Peter's Square eagerly awaiting the results of the papal conclave. It was the morning of the third day of scrutiny and the square had taken on the atmosphere of a carnival. There was singing, food, and much speculation about what was going on in the Apostolic Palace.

"Who do you think they'll choose?" I asked Guiliano.

"I have an idea, but I don't want to say," he answered coyly.

"Oh, you think you have a shot? Should I start calling you Pope Urban VII?"

As you may know, Pope Urban VI was the last pontiff to come from outside the College of Cardinals. Guiliano thought this was splendidly funny and laughed heartily, but I want to make sure you understand this reference since it's important you grasp my sense of humor and the type of playful banter Guiliano and I had with one another.

"Who is your uncle voting for?"

"Agnifilo, I think."

"Agnifilo! A Jew has a better chance at being elected."

"A Jew certainly has a better chance than a Turk. Did you hear the capitulation was mostly about the crusade against the Turks? It barely even mentioned the limits of papal authority."

"What does he see in Agnifilo?"

"Sometimes it's better to back someone you know will lose."

Guiliano was funny. Electing a pope wasn't about playing a game.

"What would you do if you were pope?" he asked me.

"Well, I'd have to lock you in a dungeon somewhere. You know too many of my secrets."

"Ah, but my uncle would pull a few strings and get me out."

"Don't be silly. I'd poison him first. You can't have any loose ends."

We shared a good laugh over this. It would be a happy memory.

Then, in that moment, I started to think about the purpose of the pope. Yes, he's the Vicar of Christ, the servant of the servants of God, the Supreme Pontiff of the Universal Church, but he's more than that, too.

"I guess I would try to unite everyone," I said solemnly, finally answering Guiliano's original question.

"Unite everyone around the idea of locking me in a dungeon?"

"No," I chuckled. "We're so divided. There are the Papal States. There's Venice and Naples."

"And the Duchies of Milan and Mantua."

"There are the Pisans."

"And the Umbrians."

"And the Florentines and the Sienese and the Ferrarese."

"Don't forget the Genovese. They hate that."

"Italy is divided and we don't have anything that could unite us," I concluded.

"And that thing can't be God?" Guiliano intimated.

"Of course it can. But it needs to be something else as well, something that we've all agreed upon and are working toward. Do you know what I mean?"

"We need a common goal," Guiliano replied, before continuing my argument. "The sciences and mathematics, art and architecture, literature, medicine and alchemy. They're all moving forward so quickly, but there's no one leader, no vision of the future tying them all together."

"I think as pope I'd try to figure out what that is," I said solemnly, perhaps a bit more seriously than was warranted.

"We should probably go tell them they need to figure that out before they finish up," Guiliano jested.

"Do you think they'll decide today?"

"I think they are getting close."

And they were.

Soon, whispers wafted through the crowd. "*Habemus Papam. Habemus Papam.*"

A pope had been chosen. But who?

"*Habemus Papam!*" A cardinal bellowed over the din of the crowd.

"I announce to you a great joy—we have a pope! The Most Eminent and Reverend Lord, Lord Francesco, Cardinal of the Holy Roman Church della Rovere, who takes to himself the name Sixtus IV."

Was I hearing him correctly? Surely the volume of his speech was not the issue, as I could hear the announcement echo off the basilica. The content itself was in question. Guiliano reassured me. The new pope was Francesco himself, Guiliano's uncle!

I don't have to tell you that there was a celebration at St. Pietro in Vincoli that night that rivaled no other I had yet experienced. Amongst the festivities, though, I started hearing rumors that not everyone was as excited about the new pontiff as I was. Apparently, against tradition, the cardinals had not made their decision unanimously. Normally, after receiving the required two-thirds vote, the other cardinals would change their votes in *accessus* to make it, at least officially, unanimous. But that didn't happen this time. I wondered why.

The rumors kept coming in the weeks following the election of Pope Sixtus IV. There were complaints of nepotism. Some were upset when he made Guiliano a cardinal and put him in charge of St. Pietro in Vincoli. They complained that Guiliano wasn't even ordained before his elevation, but they didn't know him as well as I did. Guiliano was the most pious and God-fearing man, besides the pope himself, that I had ever known.

I came to his defense as often as I could, but then something happened that made me stop. The vision of the future we talked about suddenly seemed dim.

987

Chapter Eighteen

FINDING ALBERTI

Alberti was dead.

Part of me felt as though I had died too. I couldn't do anything anymore. I had wept for Pope Paul II when he passed, but there were no tears on my pillow for Alberti. That didn't mean I could rouse myself from my bed. I laid there for days, paralyzed, my face feeling as numb as my limbs. I didn't have the energy to get up, or eat. I could not even bring myself to sleep and found myself lying awake for days in a haze of grief, my mind all but gone in my temporary insanity.

When a pope passes, there is a short period of darkness before a new candle is lit. But there would be no conclave to replace Alberti. I hope it doesn't sound sacrilegious to compare Alberti's passing to that of a pope, but he was a pillar, not only in my life, but for the greater academic community.

People had always described Alberti as a serious man. "All the rest of us to our fun and him to his books," they would say. So that's where I tried to find him after he died. I spent weeks wandering the aisles of the Vatican Library. What would his legacy be? Alberti was an intellectual giant. This library, his consultation on a project for a pope, wasn't large enough to contain a quarter of the reverence we owed him. Alberti's contributions needed to be remembered. But how? Alberti had convinced the Church to start printing books in 1467, a few years before his death, even though the Church saw the printing press as a tool of humanism, which they wanted to discourage. But they weren't printing his books, afraid to stray from Latin classic literature and ecclesiastical texts. Alberti had written truly great books, his *Della Pittura* and his treatise on cryptography, but the printer he founded would not print it and the library he designed would not carry it, at least a printed copy.

Surely, if Alberti had been there he would be able to elucidate his legacy in clear terms. He had an answer for so many things. He was the guiding force in my life, always propelling me forward, taking me first to Venice and now Rome. When I didn't know what I should do, he was always there for me. Now he was dead.

I continued skipping meals, growing weary, but hunkering down in the library nonetheless, scouring tomes for any sort of the sublime eureka that Alberti, were he alive, could have provided in an instant.

One day, I was pouring over Fibonacci's *Liber Abaci*. Like Alberti's *Della Pittura* and his *De Cifris*, Fibonacci's work was groundbreaking. One of the basic ideas he advocated for was the use of Hindu-Arabic numerals. Like many people, I now used them in my daily life due to Fibonacci's work, but many people, like Folco, still used roman numerals even though Fibonacci's book been released 300 years ago!

Surely there had been enough time for people to implement

his teachings. But they hadn't, in spite of these and Fibonacci's other, more advanced findings. Those had all fallen by the wayside. Even university curricula hadn't been set up to foster the study of mathematics. I was lucky to study under Bragadino in Venice, but most universities didn't even have a lecturer in mathematics!

I was incensed—300 years! I almost ripped *Liber Abaci* to shreds right then and there. If we didn't heed this wisdom, it should be destroyed. Better it should not exist than taunt us with our inaction. But then I seemed to hear Alberti's guiding voice, his melodious tone, or perhaps some other voice on high, imploring me to leave the tome intact.

It was then that I knew my anger had been misplaced. Yes, I was right to be angry that Fibonacci's legacy hadn't been fulfilled. I was right to be angry that Alberti's might never be, but I needed to turn my anger into impetus. The voice I heard seemed to be guiding me to a conclusion. Surely Alberti had made a bargain with God to inspire me one more time, because now I knew what I needed to do.

Alberti's contributions needed to be felt here and now. There wasn't time to wait a few more hundred years. People needed to know what he accomplished and how his work could propel all of Italy and the world forward, but they wouldn't be able to reach these conclusions on their own. They needed someone to teach and inspire them to reach for the future that this great man, these great men, promised us.

And I was the one who could do it. Now, the answer to "What should I do with my life?" was obvious. I needed to be ordained as a friar and start teaching mathematics.

I was raised by Franciscans in the Conventual order, which, as you know, allows its friars to teach. I'm friends with a cardinal, Guiliano, and the pope. They're both Franciscans in the Conventual order. I had always been deeply religious. Why had I never considered becoming a friar? It would provide a clear path to teaching.

The second step was clear, but the first less so. Becoming ordained is not a choice to be taken lightly. Although the way forward seemed obvious, I kept asking myself: should I take the cloth?

1,597

Chapter Nineteen

TWO PAINTINGS

"Put these on," Piero della Francesca ordered, handing me friar's robes. I looked at him quizzically. How did he know of my predicament?

I had traveled back to Sansepulcro. I needed time to think it over. I was only a few feet into Piero's workshop when he commandeered me to model for him. Of course, he had no idea of the decision I was contemplating. He was doing what he always did: he was working. More precisely, he was working on two paintings at the same time, the *Madonna and Child with Saints and Angels*, and the *Virgin and Child and Saints*. Both paintings featured a friar so I spent the next few days in Piero's studio posing for him, trying to remain still and quiet as a church mouse dressed in a friar's finest.

The irony of the situation was not lost on me. There I was, deciding whether or not I should take the cloth while wearing the very garment thereof. You'd think these few days of quiet contemplation would have pushed me over the edge, but they didn't. I spent most of the time trying to figure out if Piero was playing an elaborate trick on me.

Maybe it was my way of avoiding the decision. Maybe it was my way of coping. I know Alberti's death must have affected Piero too, but we didn't talk about it. Alberti only came up once. It was the last day of posing and Piero had finished both paintings. Knowing that he always had another project lined up, I asked what he was going to do next. Piero didn't need to think about it.

"I'm going to write a book on perspective in painting," he said plainly.

I was aware that Piero had made adjustments to Alberti's work on perspective. The memory of their friendly rivalry that night at dinner with the duke still provided me with amusement. But Piero had never written down his advancements.

"It's my way of making sure he isn't forgotten," Piero said.

I don't remember if I said anything in reply. If I did, it's now been forgotten. What I do remember is that these words caused joy to flood through me. Simultaneously, the full weight of Alberti's departure hit me, jolting me like a wave crashing onto the shore. My knees buckled trying to support wobbly legs. I'm old now and not ashamed to say that Piero's words released the tears I had been storing up behind my eyes. I tried to hold them back with my sleeve, but found that my tears could not be dammed.

Everything I'd done so far led me up to this moment. Fortune laid out a route in front of me and now all I was doing was recognizing it. If that moment was not a sign of my destiny then I have no idea what would have been. I was resolute. Then, more than ever.

I'd taken the time necessary to fully envisage my decision, as the young man transcribing my words surely must, if he has not already done so.

I knew I had to answer God's call and become a friar.

2,584

Chapter Twenty

BROTHERS

"Brother!"

My eyes lit up. It couldn't be. The voice I heard was new, but I swore I could place it. Two men appeared before me as I entered the monastery in Sansepulcro, welcoming me to the first day of my novitiate, the first day on my long journey to becoming a friar. While their current forms were foreign to me, their identities shone brightly behind their eyes.

"Guinipero? Ambrogio!" I cried out.

Here they were, my two nephews! My brother Piero's sons. Although they were my nephews, in reality they were more like brothers to me. This is not only due to our proximity in age, but in the bond we developed over the course of my novitiate. Guinipero and Ambrogio were already friars at the monastery. How had I not known this? I had expected to see them in town, but not as friars!

My heart felt like it was dancing on the moon. I found that I was crying, but these were no longer tears of anguish, but rather tears of joy. The concept of joy had seemed foreign to me for far too long and I was more than happy to be able to turn my gray skies blue.

Their warm welcome remains as one of the most delightful surprises of my life. The two young men guided me on my novitiate, providing a constant source of companionship, guidance and wisdom. They became my brothers, not only in cloth, but also in spirit. Or rather, in spirit beyond the traditional fraternal order.

I trained and prepared for life as a friar. I learned to become the man I am today. The narcissism that made me unaware of my brothers' ordination was removed from me. I don't want to go into much more detail in front of the young man transcribing my words. Each novitiate's journey is unique and I wouldn't want to color his inculcation with tales of my own.

The most important thing is that it gave me time to reflect. It deepened my resolve. I knew what God's purpose was for me.

4,181

Chapter Twenty-One

THE FIRST

My mouth was open, but no words were coming out. Although I knew God's purpose for me, it wasn't always easy to execute His vision. I stood, uneasily still, as if I were a woodland fawn my students had wandered across. To that degree, I played my part, trying to make as little motion as possible. Trying as hard as I could to get them not to notice me so that they might pass by and leave me unmolested.

It was my first day lecturing at the University of Perugia. Guiliano had put in a good word for me. He had studied the sciences there while he was a cleric in the monastery nearby, but there probably was one cardinal reason his recommendation led to my position: his Cardinalship.

As you know, students rely on lectures from their professors to gain knowledge and insight into their intended subject. Although I had been studying mathematics for years, I hadn't yet thought to practice this part of the profession. There were no longer just two sets of eager eyes staring back at me, like there had been with the Rompiasi boys. Now, there were dozens. It was paralyzing. I could foretell that no great wisdom would pass between minds today. My silence was letting them down. I needed to command their attention, like Bragadino had done for me, enrapturing me with his accumulated knowledge. I needed to speak with gravity and verve. I needed to perform.

But those eyes. The penetrating eyes of my students. The eyes that seemed to cut into my soul and damn me as an aberration not fit to stand in front of them, let alone teach them. There were so many of them, I found it hard enough to keep my head up, let alone venture to speak.

As I was building up my courage, a question from my audience snapped me out of my nervous coma.

"What's going to happen next year?"

"Let us first begin with this year's curriculum," I answered.

"No," another student retorted. "What's going to happen next year? Is there going to be another war? An earthquake perhaps?"

Now I understood their query. They weren't asking a question about mathematics, the future of knowledge, they were asking about the perceptible future, as if I were a common soothsayer and not a mathematician. I should have expected their ignorance. It was not uncommon at the time for mathematicians to dabble in astrology, even though it was a bastard science. As I was the first lecturer in mathematics at the University of Perugia, there was bound to be the occasional confusion.

"Astrology is pagan and ungodly," I retorted. "We will only study mathematics here."

In hindsight, I probably could have found a better way to inform my students of this. Perhaps it was this response, or my stilted lecturing, but I lost half of my students that day, most of them never to return. I tried to gain them back, trying to be a better lecturer, but it was a slow slog. With astrology out of the picture, I didn't have much with which to entice them back. It didn't help that the most popular subjects at the time, law and medicine, both remunerated their students well upon graduation. Students didn't even need to look far for examples—they needed only look to their lecturers. My colleagues lecturing in medicine earned 1,000 ducats a year in salary compared to my relatively paltry 40 ducats. Were twenty-five of me really worth only one of them? Apparently the University thought so in their analysis.

The students didn't linger far behind. I was now left with only a handful of faithful pupils and trying to tempt more to join their ranks was a difficult problem. In order to solve it, I first attempted to remove myself from the equation. I reached out to old friends, including my dear Antonio Cornaro who was still studying mathematics, attempting to see if there was a textbook or some other manual that I could teach from. My thinking was that the students would never learn anything from my unpolished stammering so they should at least be given some resource to glean from. Yes, I had produced the manuals for the Rompiasi boys, but I had stupidly given them up in an ascetic exercise during my novitiate. Not that anything done on your novitiate is stupid, mind you. Just my implementation of certain rules, not having fully realized yet that books are a necessity and not an indulgence.

Their replies to my query came fast. I was so excited. Now, finally, I could start properly teaching my students! But their replies didn't carry good news. They all confirmed that there was no textbook in mathematics that I could use. There was Euclid's *Elements*, but it was only available in Ancient Greek.

So I set upon the arduous task of recreating the manuals on

geometry, algebra, and the Venetian double-entry bookkeeping method that I had done before. I thought they might even come out better this time now, though, since I now possessed an even greater mastery of the subject. I worked quickly, preferring the strain of authorship to the anxiety of professorship.

I expected my manuals to be a rousing success. And I thought they were. I had my students pass around and copy my first manual on geometry before my next lecture. When I came to class, all had a fresh version in front of them. As I began the lecture, I noticed that my students' heads were buried in their manuals. They weren't looking at me! I could feel the pressure melting off my back.

I was exultant and stood tall. I lectured, well, professorially, trying to emulate Bragadino. I could see the path ahead clearly. My students would gather the primary points from my manuals. I wouldn't have to double these points in my lecture. Rather, I could illustrate these points using real-world examples. I could regale them with anecdotes while having a sturdy foundation to fall back on. If I faltered in my lecturing, I would simply move on to the next subject in the manual, my students following closely behind.

It all seemed perfect. I spoke sanguinely that day, confidently orating the story of Plato emblazoning "Let no one ignorant of geometry enter" above the door of his academy. I wasn't far into this story, though, when I could sense that my students were not following along. They were more confused than ever. That's when I realized that I was lecturing in Latin, but I'd written the manual in Italian! The students were struggling as they juggled two languages at once. Trying to understand the principles I'd written down for them in one language and my anecdote in another. I was barely one day into this new experiment and was already failing.

My folly was understandable, though. Latin was the lingua franca of academics. All the professors, including me, were expected to lecture in Latin. I could have easily written my manual in the language, and presumed I would if it was the hit I expected it to be, but it hadn't occurred to me to produce this new first draft in Latin. I wrote my previous manuals in Italian. Alberti wrote *Della Pittura* in Italian before he produced a Latin translation as well and that was a success. I thought my trajectory would be the same.

I apologized to my students. It wasn't reasonable for them to have to parse two tongues at once in order to understand my lectures. But that left me with a decision. Should I continue lecturing in Latin and have all their eyes upon me again? Or should I do the unthinkable . . . and lecture in Italian?

It had always been hard to talk about mathematics in Latin. Latin was a constant, fixed language, whereas Italian, like mathematics itself, was constantly changing. It was, at once, both an easy and a very difficult decision to make. I didn't know what the university would say if I broke precedent and lectured to my students in Italian. They might fire me. If they did, they would have had good cause. At the same time though, I didn't know what would happen to me and my anxiety if I had to continue enduring the direct attention of my students.

In that moment, I grappled hard with my decision. What should I do? What would Alberti do? What would Piero do? Piero, I believed, planned to write his update to Alberti's tome exclusively in Italian, finding it difficult to fully explain his new concepts in the old language. That settled it for me. Latin is the language of the past. Italian and mathematics are the languages of the future.

Thus, I jeopardized my teaching position. I became the first professor at the University of Perugia to lecture in Italian. Luckily, it paid off—my style was a hit. When my lectures were less than dazzling, my manuals picked up the slack. I was so much more articulate on the page than in person.

Students flocked to my class, and more importantly, mathematics. Apparently, their fear of missing something in other professor's lectures was as great as my fear of leaving something out. When studying for my classes, they no longer had to question their notes, pondering over whether they had taken down my lecture exactly as I'd said it. They didn't have to pray their recollections were not false prophets. They had my teachings in front of them, direct from my brain to theirs.

I soon wrote quite a collection of manuals. I followed up geometry with algebra and then merchant arithmetic. I wrote about barter, exchange, and the Venetian double-entry bookkeeping method, as I had done before. I even wrote one on how to mix metals, since calculations needed to be precise in that regard. My collection grew until they added up to almost 600 pages, an impressive amount of work that I would never again discard in an ascetic relapse. And I couldn't even if I wanted to, since my students had made sure copies were commonplace, at least at the university.

I combined all of these manuals into my first textbook, a manuscript that I dubbed the *Tractatus mathematicus ad discipulos perusinos* (*Treaty on mathematics to my students in Perugia*). I was proud of it, of course. I dedicated the manuscript to my students at Perugia, especially the handful who remained faithful to me after my stunted beginning. My following had grown over the course of those four years. By the time I left, I had nearly 150 students. As my classes grew larger, my nerves seemed to shrink. I never developed into a lecturer of Bragadino's caliber, but I could command an audience.

I came to enjoy lecturing. After a while, it was a hunger that I looked forward to feeding. One day, though, my appetite started getting the best of me. I knew I was connecting with my students, but I felt like there was something bigger that I needed to do, that there was some other missing piece to God's puzzle for me.

I could have continued at my current pace and been quite happy, but I knew that I needed to reach more students than my position in Perugia would allow. I was the only lecturer in mathematics at my university and most still didn't even have one. It was a problem and I needed to solve it.

For the first time in my life, I didn't look to others to help me make my decision. I didn't look to Alberti or Piero. I knew what I needed to do.

6,765

Transcriber's note: After Fra. Pacioli transcribed this chapter to me, he wanted to make sure to remind him to return to it in the future, as to possibly amend his testimony on the usefulness of Latin. As best I remember, I believe his reasoning to me was thus, "Although Latin is not the language of science and mathematics, there is a certain poetry that arises when something is communicated in a language that is not a common tongue. It's almost as if the knowledge of one's ancestors were being dredged like a canal."

Chapter Twenty-Two

THE FLOWER OF THE WORLD

Florence was the flower of the world. The sciences, business, and art were all blossoming there. I knew that I had to become a magister, to achieve the highest level of education in my field. There was no better place to do that than in Florence, the center of everything.

My greatest happiness, though, was that I was not alone on this journey. My old mathematician friend Antonio Cornaro was in Florence, too, and we were both determined to achieve our magister. We spent our days studying like good schoolboys, but just as Antonio had introduced me to the grand life in Venice, he and his family's name ushered me into social circles in Florence that I might not have had entrée to otherwise.

One particular night from this period stands out. Perhaps it was the opulent setting or how an exchange with one great painter ended up shaping my future with another, but I will never forget the night Sandro Botticelli stood with his arms outstretched, welcoming me with a hug into his home.

The only peculiarity in this situation was that I had never met the man. I thought I would just be one of many guests at a party he was throwing in honor of a new painting he had completed. I had secured my invitation through my acquaintance with Antonio, but until that moment, I didn't know the conditions under which my invitation had been produced.

Apparently, Antonio had met Botticelli earlier and sang my praises. He mentioned that I used to apprentice with Piero della Francesca and I used to work for Leon Battista Alberti. Antonio probably would have said that I'd worked for the pope if he thought it would secure my invitation. Although, now that I think about it, I did work for the pope, albeit slightly indirectly in my position as Alberti's assistant. I mean, I know the pope and consider him a friend, but wouldn't think of mentioning that myself. It is moments like this that show how much I have trouble capitalizing on my associations in the way that some men do for social advantage. Luckily, I had Antonio in my life to do it for me.

Botticelli was very enthusiastic in his greeting.

"A fellow artist!" he proclaimed out of a false sense of shared purpose and too much wine.

Apparently, Antonio had sold him a bag of false goods. I scoured my brain for the best way to diffuse his excitement, but he was much too determined to pause for my penitence. I didn't want to say something in the moment that might cause him to escort me to the street for an even more private party, one all by myself.

"Let me show it to you," he slurred as he grabbed my arm, luring me into his abode.

There were a lot of interesting persons at this gala. A lot of people I should have liked to meet if I were not being dragged past them. A gaggle of rowdy children frolicked amongst the revelers, seemingly in the midst of their own Battle of the Stones.

"My brother's children. So many of them!" Botticelli complained. "They want to kick me out! Make me go back to my studio at the Medici's, but you know what I say to that?"

But I had no time to respond. Our arrival at his painting cut short any potential reply and distracted him from his dissatisfaction.

"Behold!" he bellowed.

I was confronted with a naked woman. On canvas, that is. Botticelli's painting was of the most dazzlingly beautiful woman, naked, standing or slightly hovering above a clamshell. Two entwined beings blew her onto shore where another woman waited to cover up her immodesty.

"That's not Eve," I said, confused.

Up until this point in time, if a nude woman was portrayed in a painting it was always Eve, who was, of course, as naked as God made her in the Garden of Eden. Outside of an ancient bawdy vase or whorehouse wall, not that I would have any direct knowledge thereof, no one had painted nude women for quite some time. Here was something drastically fresh and here I was a newly ordained friar, one of the first men to gaze upon her sumptuous curves.

"It's Venus," Botticelli revealed. "I was basing it off a Roman sculpture, but then I discovered that sculpture was based on a Greek one. Now that was something to see."

I was impressed. His mind seemed to work like mine. His inspiration had its source in another work and he took the time to track it down, analyze it, and make it his own. It's the type of work that Piero della Francesca was doing as well. I thought this was perhaps another great man I could learn from and support.

"That's what I do," I told him excitedly. "I research ancient wisdom and try to make it new again. Tell me, what was Greece like?"

"Greece? Ah, you mean the statue. Didn't have to go. The Medici family bought it. It's here. In Florence. Those bastards, they are buying all the best art in the world, including this," Botticelli said, referencing his painting.

"What do you think?" he asked me, smiling widely, seemingly already sure of the answer I'd give.

I thought about it for a moment. I wanted to impress him. I didn't want to be just another one in a parade of sycophants at the party, trotting out their praises without truly appreciating and analyzing his work.

"It's mesmerizing," I said. "But flat."

"What do you mean, flat?"

"The linear perspective. The shoreline. It's supposed to go off into the distance, but right now, well, did you use a perspective grid?"

Of course he didn't. That much was obvious. It was a rhetorical question, but even if I had been looking for an answer, Botticelli didn't seem too keen to provide one. I feared my strategy was failing so I tried to set his mind at ease.

"Don't worry, it doesn't look like it would take much work to rework it and get it right. You wouldn't have to repaint Venus or the other figures, just the background. And since the background is pretty simple and there's a clear distinction between background and foreground it shouldn't take you too long. I can help you out with the perspective grid, of course. It's my specialty."

"Your specialty as an artist is perspective grids?"

I knew it was now or never. I needed to clear the air about

my limitations as an artist if I hoped to turn this situation around and gain Botticelli's trust.

"Yes. I'm humble enough to admit that whatever talent I have as an artist is confined within this relatively limited scope. I apprenticed with Piero della Francesca and Alberti, but at an early age I found that I have no talent with the brush. What skill I do possess is with the plummet line and compass, assisting other artists produce natural backgrounds in their work."

"So, you are not an artist."

"I'm a mathematician. But in this regard, it would be my highest honor to help you. To make the painting more realistic."

"Realistic? It's Venus. She's standing on a giant clamshell. It's not supposed to be realistic."

"I only mean the perspective."

"But you're not an artist."

"I permit that may color my attention."

"I just finished a commission at the Vatican you know. Pope Sixtus IV himself relished my work."

"Francesco. Yes. I mean Sixtus IV. A great man. I lived with him and his nephew for a while. I'm curious, though, what did Guiliano, Cardinal della Rovere, think? He has more of a background in the sciences than his uncle."

"I don't need to explain my work to you. Anyway, you wouldn't understand if you tried. There's often pushback from the uninitiated when someone breaks boundaries. I'm the first painter to present Venus, the epitome of the female form, in all her glory."

"And she is overwhelming in her beauty. If a woman existed who could make me renounce my vows as a friar, it would be she," I said, cutting my losses.

Botticelli considered me for a moment, then smiled.

"There may be hope for you yet."

My relief was great. It was so great, in fact, that I felt compelled to hug him. Luckily, as a friar, I could get away this kind of friendly activity. As we embraced, my head fell back, allowing me a brief glimpse upward to heaven, thanking God for my deliverance out of this situation.

Perhaps it was my youthful insolence slipping past my tongue again, the kind of narcissism I thought I had removed from my conscious mind during my novitiate, or perhaps it was because I had, in the end, transformed into the type of sycophant I derided, but for some reason when I let go of him I felt the need to follow up my previous compliment.

"Artists have been getting perspective wrong in painting for years, though. There's nothing new in that."

If my previous line seemed to get me back into Botticelli's good graces, this last one secured his disdain for me, in addition to my dis-invitation to any future gatherings. That night's was the first and last parties of his that I attended.

While it stung, I didn't have too much time to linger on it. Although Antonio and I occasionally dabbled in the entertainments of the city, we spent most of our time in Florence working on our magisters. We studied in the library at St. Marks, the one that Cosimo Medici built before his death. It contained a trove of tomes on mathematics in Latin and Greek. They had *Witelo's Perspectiva*, the same book that Alberti told me about all those years back in Urbino. More impressively, though, they had a copy of the Latin version of the book that *Witelo's Perspectiva* was based upon, the *Kitab al-manazir*, which contained key texts on optics and perspective by the Arab mathematician Ibn al-Haytham.

Although I had not yet passed through that angelic gate, the one made out of a single pearl, I was in heaven. Luckily I didn't have to spend much time outside this veritable kingdom since I was able to secure lodging at St. Marks in the apartment of a reverend cardinal there. My days were focused on using what little sense God had given me, achieving a modicum of result, but progressing nonetheless.

I had been quite fortunate in my life, first gaining entrance to the library in Urbino, then the Vatican, and now St. Marks. It was a level of access that most people would never possess. I was proud of this achievement, but mindful of its implication. My students needed to gain the wisdom and accumulated knowledge of places like this, but there was perhaps not even a single young person in the world who had the time and resources to replicate my path, venturing from library to library, soaking up the wisdom of the ages.

In this way, my pride guided me back to my purpose.

10,946

Chapter Twenty-Three

GUIDOBALDO

I needed to get back to my students and the University of Perugia was happy to have me. I didn't need Guiliano's recommendation this time around. I had the reputation I built before my departure and my newly minted magister to vouch for me.

Rather, it was I who needed to give something to Guiliano: my condolences. Pope Sixtus IV, his uncle, my dear patron and host, our dear Francesco, was dead. I returned to Rome and we laid him to rest in his tomb in the choir chapel at St. Peter's.

As you may remember, even though Francesco was finally at rest, the city was not. A mob descended like a plague on the palace of Girolamo Riario, one of Francesco's other nephews. The locusts stripped his home. No furniture left on the floor. The walls were as bare as the affront. Even the garden was destroyed. Trees lay sad and uprooted, as if sympathizing with their owner.

Guiliano and I were busy trying to beat back a mob, albeit one comprised of papal officials, all of whom were intent on taking tokens of their deceased pontiff. Mourners marauded around the papal palace, nabbing knick-knacks, and desks, and, well, anything they could get their hands on when we weren't looking.

The looting got so bad that Johann Burchard, the indomitable master of ceremonies, complained to us that there were no towels or linens to use to bathe Francesco's body. And even if there were, all of his shirts and drawers had been taken as well, so there was not an article of his own clothing to bury him in. This put Johann and Guiliano in quite the predicament, forcing them to bury Francesco quickly, and unfortunately, unceremoniously. It was an indignity undeserving of such of a great man.

I knew Guiliano was in a great deal of pain over this. I entreated him to confide in me, but he would not. It seemed like it was hard for him to speak. Sometimes I would catch him muttering under his breath, enigmatically, "The Borgias . . ."

Knowing how much his uncle meant to him, I vowed to Guiliano that I would stay with him until his wounds healed. Despite my protestations, Guiliano, or should I say Cardinal della Rovere as was his title at the time, made it clear that while he appreciated my concern, it was not required.

Finally, when Guiliano broke his silence he said, in his words, "I will honor him in the best way I know how—by continuing the work to which he dedicated his life."

I immediately understood. It was precisely the same logic I used to simultaneously mourn and celebrate Alberti.

On my way back to Perugia, I decided to stop by the library in Urbino. It was to be part of my homecoming tour. I wanted to revisit the library in which I spent so much time in as a young man, the first library to whet my appetite for those hallowed grounds. When I arrived at the library, though, I was surprised to find that some people didn't share my reverence for these institutions, or so it seemed.

The pristine order of the shelves had been disrupted. Previously, every book was meticulously cataloged. Every book had a place on the shelf and there was a place for every book. Now, books lay strewn across the tables. There were tall stacks that could have blotted out the sun if it had been shining in the room. These towers threatened to teeter, fall over, and crush anyone who disturbed them.

The librarian I remembered was nowhere to be seen. The only sign of life was a small tuft of hair sticking up over a short wall of books. I circled the table, scaling the walls he had built up around himself, to find a boy a few years younger than I had been when I was first granted access to the library. Immediately, I assumed his entrée was similar to mine.

"What are you reading?" I asked, hoping to spark a conversation and encourage the boy.

He didn't respond. He didn't even acknowledge my presence.

"What are you reading?" I asked again, my patience straining a bit.

That's when the boy turned on me, his lips curling. "Who are you? Who said you could come in here?"

I smiled. "I'm Luca Pacioli and Piero della Francesca arranged my access with the duke himself."

"Piero della Francesca? If you know him then you must know his work on the five regular solids," the boy said as he slammed the book shut and slid it toward me.

I kept calm, not wanting to give credence to his impetuousness by acknowledging it. Also, I had made the mistake of saying it had been Piero who had asked the duke for my access, when it had in fact been Alberti. And I wanted neither of these to show on my face. But I couldn't help but be perplexed. The book was not one I recognized even though it had Piero della Francesca's name on it. The boy must have noticed my surprise.

"It's a new book," he said.

Indeed, it must have been. It was a treatise on the five regular solids, the work that Piero dedicated himself to after Alberti's death. I sat down to start delving into the book's treasures, but noticed something curious in its opening pages. The book was dedicated to the Duke of Urbino. Now, that part of it was unsurprising. The two had long had jovial personal and professional relationship. What surprised me was the name he gave to the duke. It said, "Dedicated to the Duke of Urbino, Guidobaldo da Montefeltro," not Federico as it should have been.

"What is the origination of this book?" I asked suspiciously as I held the offending page in front of the boy's eyes, pointing at it. "There is a typographical error."

"No, there's not."

I pointed at it again, this time tapping my finger for emphasis. "Right here. It says the book is dedicated to . . ."

"I know," the boy bellowed, cutting me off.

"Well then, that . . ."

"That's me. I'm Guidobaldo da Montefeltro. I'm the Duke of Urbino. Who are you really? How did you get in here?"

I was dumbstruck. I didn't know how to answer his questions. The boy was not simply a visitor to the library, he was its patron.

Guidobaldo took my silence as evidence of incapacitation of another kind and asked, "Are you drunk?"

Truthfully, though I was not, I felt like I was. It was the second time in my life that I had made a complete ass out of myself in that library.

"But then that means . . ." I stammered.

I looked to Guidobaldo for answers, but his eyes were so gaunt, simultaneously answering my question and begging me not to ask it.

I was asking this boy to conjure the memory of his father's death. How could I be so unthinking? And how had I not known about this? Had I been so consumed with Francesco's death that I hadn't heard of Federico's? Even if I had been, it didn't excuse my rudeness.

I sat down and apologized to him. I closed my eyes and tried to connect his heart to mine, hoping that God might allow me to take on some of this boy's hurt.

"I'm sorry. You shouldn't have to bear my ignorant folly."

Having just consoled Guiliano about Francesco, I attempted to console Guidobaldo about Federico. I spoke about my relationship to Piero and later Alberti, and how hard it had been to lose him and the guidance he provided. We found common ground in Piero, who had been advising the young Guidobaldo. Apparently, Piero saw enough in the young man to dedicate his new work to him. As our conversation meandered, I learned that Guidobaldo had clearly ingested the lessons of the book along with those of other scholars in literature and warfare as well.

Guidobaldo wanted to prove everyone wrong who doubted that someone so young could rule wisely, and at still only thirteen years old, he had a lot to prove. He had been using the library as his personal study, trying to become a master of all the knowledge therein. I wanted to do everything I could to help this young beneficent scholar on his journey and immediately had the opportunity to put this desire into practice.

Guidobaldo lamented that there was no one book he could turn to in mathematics, no one book to give an overview of the various fields that could jumpstart his studies in each one of them. Rather, he had to pull from multiple sources, always hoping he was building a faultless overview of the discipline in his head.

While I didn't have a copy with me, I promised to send him my *Tractatus mathematicus ad discipulos perusinos*, the collection of manuals in mathematics I made for my students in Perugia.

Ah, my students. I still needed to get back to them. Most, nay, not a single one would ever have the resources that Guidobaldo had in front of him. They didn't have their own fully stocked libraries or access to the ones that exist.

They needed me to bring this knowledge to them.

17,711

Chapter Twenty-Four

ROUND TWO

I fed off Guidobaldo's passion. The world was truly changing. Young people like him were eager to learn mathematics and I was all too eager to fulfill their desire. I fell back into the rhythm of teaching in Perugia. My lectures were emphatic as before. I had seen even more of the world and I used even more real-world examples to engage my students.

I told them the story of the twins. The story the merchant Onofofrio Oini related about a dying man who wanted to make a will. His wife was with child and he wanted the will to be different depending on whether the child was a boy or a girl. That was all well and good until the baby was born. Or rather, babies. Twins to be precise—a boy and a girl. The will couldn't be altered since the man had already died, before the children were born. You could take his will to a lawyer, but since there had been no precedent for this situation, one had to look outside the profession for answers.

So, how should his will be interpreted?

First, I would let my students stew over this, encouraging their minds to ponder the dilemma. Then, after batting down hopeful but incorrect solutions, I'd reveal the Rule of Three. We knew the man's assets, how he would divide them if his progeny were male, and how that would be altered if it were female. We know these three terms and we need to deduce the division of assets, or rather, the fourth term.

Using the Rule of Three, the fourth term is a simple proportion that can be deduced by the ratios between the other three where: If $a/b = c/x$. Then $x = bc/a$.

The teaching style I was developing helped students absorb the material and see its application beyond the problem in front of them. I would use the commercial concepts they were more familiar with to illustrate mathematical principles. These principles then showed, as they do in this example of the man's will, how their logic could be applied to other fields including the law, which still might pay better wages but can't be applied to many other areas of study.

I spent the next six years of my life in this mode, lecturing to each new crop of students, hoping my lectures would spark the flame of knowledge I knew was inside them. I would use examples as soon as I noticed they struggled to engage with the material. I even started using a new game called chess to demonstrate mathematical principles and logic.

I was now the teacher I had wanted to become all those years before. The teacher I envisioned as Piero made me stand still in friar's robes, posing for those two paintings. How fond that memory was now. I was now a much older man—forty-six to be precise—than the twenty-six-year-old boy who modeled for Piero all those years before.

Piero was then a much older man too, seventy-seven to be precise, so I shouldn't have been surprised when tragedy struck.

28,657

Chapter Twenty-Five

THE REBIRTH

As a man of God, I've thought much about my own mortality and that of others. But I found myself wholly unprepared to handle losing the second and last great mentor of my life, Piero della Francesca.

His passing hit me hard. I could feel the desire to cower in my bed creeping into my bones. Comfort could be found there, and quiet and rest. I could pretend that it hadn't happened. I could pretend that I wasn't alone.

Surely, I had lost a mentor before, my dear Alberti, so I had some idea on how best to cope, or at least the emotional journey thereof, but the last time I faced such a venture I had another mentor to guide me, Piero himself. Now, I had no one. No one, that is, besides Guidobaldo, who lovingly commiserated with me.

Guidobaldo was now twenty years old. We drank in Piero's accomplishments, discussing his work over some sorely needed wine. In addition to Piero's many painted works, some of which were in Guidobaldo's collection, he had also completed books on perspective and that one about the five regular solids that he had dedicated to Guidobaldo. Both were completed after Alberti's death, ignited by a bright flame that had gone out.

Now, the torch had been passed to me. There's nothing like the death of your idols to light a fire within your soul.

I began working like a mad man. Inspired by Isidore, the first Christian writer to compile a *summa* of universal knowledge a millennia ago . . . inspired by Nicomachus who summarized the accumulated knowledge of mathematics in the first century . . . inspired by Piero and Alberti . . . inspired by my students at University and the countless other students I couldn't reach directly . . . inspired by a young Guidobaldo scouring multiple books in his library trying to learn mathematics . . . inspired by the same craving I saw in his eyes as an adult, I saw something grand and magnificent.

While Guidobaldo had grown into quite a leader, and his eyes were no longer gaunt, I could see that they were still haunted by the legacy, but not by ghosts who wished to dispense anguish. Rather, Guidobaldo was haunted by the pleasant spirit that is the accumulated knowledge of the great men who came before him and the inherent duress that the guardianship of such a spirit entails.

Although Guidobaldo's face was much fairer than mine, due in no small part to the twenty-six additional rings I possess around my trunk, it felt like I was looking in a mirror as we remembered our mutual mentor. Our sage. Our Piero. I was not alone.

It was there, deep within his eyes, that I saw an opportunity.

46,368

Chapter Twenty-Six

THE SUM

I pitched a book to Aldus Manutius, one of the biggest printers in Venice. I had finished a manuscript and now wanted to make a printed mathematical textbook that would contain the sum of all mathematical knowledge known at the time. We would call it the *Summa de arithmetica, geometria, proportioni et proportionalita* (*Summary of arithmetic, geometry, proportions and proportionality*). No longer would students have to find and read multiple books just to get an overview. No longer would they have to write down everything their teacher said and rely on the quality of the teacher to convey complex concepts. No longer would only my students at the University of Perugia be given these gifts. My *Summa* would be a text that all students can use to teach themselves. And the printing press would allow it to be distributed far and wide.

I was confident that Aldus would instantly embrace my proposal. Up until recently, book publishing had been dominated by religious texts and Latin classics. Unlike fruit sellers, who can expect repeat business from their customers who buy the same product day after day, booksellers sell a product that will often outlive its owner. So, after an initial surge in business, booksellers and printers saw their profits decline.

But printers like Aldus, being the businessmen that they are, had stumbled across a new, unexpected market: instructional books. Thousands of printed books were flooding the marketplace, on topics ranging from how to play musical instruments to how to sew garments.

Information that was previously only available to small groups of people was now open to everyone. Regrettably, even in the midst of this explosion, Aldus didn't think there would be demand for a book about mathematics, or as he called it, "numbers and such," and he turned me down.

Fortunately, there were now more than 100 other printers in Venice. Unfortunately, nearly all of them turned me down as well. Or, they would agree to the printing as long as I covered the costs associated with its production. Now, as a friar, I was more a man of access than a man of means, so this proposition held the same functional value as an outright refusal.

The printing itself would be relatively inexpensive, mind you. While it cost three times as much to set up and print a book than to have a scribe duplicate the same work, you could print 1,000 copies on a printing press with the same amount of money, whereas the scribe could only make one. I think I told you that already, but it's worth repeating.

Regardless, let it suffice to say that I could not afford to hire three scribes. As much as I've discussed my love for books, you may have assumed that I had scribes transcribing them for me constantly, but truthfully, I don't think I would have purchased books even if I had been able to afford them, preferring the edition and environment the library provides. In this way, my poverty was a welcome restriction.

I sought solace for my predicament with my old friend Antonio Cornaro, who had taken over the position of public lecturer in mathematics at Scuola di Rialto from our illustrious professor and predecessor Bragadino. It was an enviable position, but I couldn't have been happier to see my friend's professional role now match his social and familial one.

Being a man about town, Antonio introduced me to Marco Sanuto, another professor in mathematics at the Scuola di Rialto and a member of the famous Sanuto family. Together, we three opined about how sorely this textbook was needed in order to push our field forward. As the night went on, our opining transitioned into exploration. We traipsed through the canals, haunting the establishments from our happy youth. For the city of Venice, sleep seemed to be a choice and not a necessity. There was always something to see and do at any time of the night. As was our custom, I paid what I could for our adventures and Antonio covered the rest, adding it to the ever-expanding ledger that I knew he would never total.

Perhaps Marco noticed this, or perhaps our evening's enchantments were still transfixing him, but as we were saying our goodbyes and good mornings the next day, something wonderful happened that, beyond its immediate impact, perhaps illustrates the gulf between someone like myself and my new dear pal Marco Sanuto.

As we relinquished his tired body over his threshold to the waiting arms of his family, Marco turned to Antonio and me and said, "Why don't I just pay for it?"

75,025

Chapter Twenty-Seven

THE FINE PRINT

O nce the printing of my *Summa* was funded, it didn't take long for me to find a willing printer. I chose the affable Paganino de Paganini to do the work. I'd tell you how much Marco contributed to the process, but Paganini wouldn't like me sharing that information with those outside his profession. Suffice to say, we could afford to print an astounding 1,500 books in the first run!

I should have been paying Paganini room and board. I was at his workshop day and night. Or perhaps, he should have paid me a wage. I would proofread the typesetting and rectify errors with my own hand. It was an unpaid apprenticeship, but unlike my previous situation with Folco, this was one I toiled at with gusto.

The book had to be done right. It combined all the knowledge I'd gained over the years. I had studied Euclid's *Elements*, Jacobus Cremonensis' translation of Archimedes, the algebra of al-Khwarizmi and other Arab scholars, and, of course the work on mathematical and artistic perspective by Leon Battista Alberti and Piero della Francesca. Perhaps more so than any other work, though, I absorbed Fibonacci's *Liber Abaci*. If any concept in my *Summa* is not sourced to another scholar, it can surely be attributed to Fibonacci and his seminal work.

I had been studying the entire body of mathematics for twenty years at the world's greatest libraries. And now I was in the position to summarize all this knowledge and educate those new to the subject in the way that only an experienced teacher such as myself could do. I was going to combine all these sources, because like Fibonacci's numbers, one thought springs from another, and together their sum increases.

If a printer had taken up the task of printing the manuals for the Rompiasi boys I made all those years ago, the total sum of the knowledge contained in those books would be much less than it is today. And we wouldn't have had the ability to properly print Hindu-Arabic numerals. The technology to print these figures accurately was only invented about ten years prior to my *Summa*, around the same time Paganini opened his shop.

If only Vitruvius had been able to print precise figures, he wouldn't have had to roll around in his grave for a few centuries until someone was finally able to crack the secret of Vitruvian proportionality and circle his square. But I digress—that's something I'll get into more depth later when I discuss my time with Leonardo.

Now, only a decade after printing precise figures was made possible, my *Summa* was going to be the first printed book to deal with Hindu-Arabic arithmetic. And while I'm proud of every portion of the book, there's one particular section that has a very important place in my heart.

121,393

Chapter Twenty-Eight

ON COMPUTING

I called it *De computis*, or *On computing*. In addition to being the first printed book to deal with Hindu-Arabic arithmetic, my *Summa* was the first printed book to codify the double-entry bookkeeping method. It was the system I learned in Venice and wished I had had earlier, when I was in Folco's shop.

Other mathematicians may not have thought to incorporate a section on bookkeeping into a book on mathematics, but to me, its inclusion couldn't be more significant. While mathematicians toil away in libraries and universities, the businessmen of this world labor on land and sea. They sell their wares in peacetime and wartime alike, in times of health and in pestilence. Businessmen are the cornerstones of republics.

Merchants are exactly the people I wanted to read this book. Yes, the book did well with my students, but if I could explain the system of double-entry bookkeeping clearly enough, merchants all across Europe would start using it. And thus, by incorporating a bookkeeping section, the other mathematical concepts would be propelled forward along with it.

I learned arithmetic in the context of training for the business trade. I knew that there was an intellectual army of merchant clerks who were ready to be activated, called up for service. This section was my Trojan horse, the one that would gain access for all the others.

In this way, I knew my *Summa* might uncover a hidden source of intelligence. It was not only important for the merchants to possess a good knowledge of bookkeeping, but for their wives as well. As you know, merchants frequently undergo long periods of traveling and it's important that their wives keep accurate records while they are away. Therefore, women would be introduced to the broad set of mathematical concepts as well, assuming they chose to peruse those parts of the book.

I poured my heart and soul into it. It was a gargantuan task, combining the world's mathematical knowledge into one volume, but to that degree, there is only chaos in the world without order and I was bringing order to it.

I was exhausted when we finished the first print run, but it was the type of fatigue that follows swimming in a mountain lake. My body was tired, but my mind was invigorated and soaring.

Folco joked with me. "You are now the father of accounting."

"No, I'm not the father. I am the midwife," I corrected. "*We* are the midwives, encouraging its birth."

In truth, there is only one father of accounting and that is the Heavenly Father. Now, if for some reason you've forgotten that I'm a friar, let me share my sermon with you. For this is the real reason that this section is important to me, not only as a teacher and mathematician, but as a child and disciple of the Holy Father.

It is at times like this when Matthew 6:33 looms large in my mind. "But seek ye first the kingdom of God, and his righteousness; and all these things shall be added unto you."

Everything that each of us does—whether a washerwoman or an artist, a banker or a bureaucrat—should be done in service to God. I give advice and wisdom on how to balance ledgers, but it is all in service of being the most faithful servant and training others to do their best under His stewardship.

Engaging members of the business community in these dictums was sometimes onerous, but being the resourceful friar I am, I would often employ their own ego in the quest to save their souls. For it was Paul the Apostle who exhorted his adherents that to be worthy of the crown you must fight readily for it. It was commonplace for local merchants to swear upon the names of the Medici or other large banking families who have accumulated wealth and esteem. Is it not blasphemy for them to do this, you might ask? No, it is not and hereby do I explain my logic. One supports the other, a business builds and supports a republic. It does the heavenly work of decreasingly income disparity, the work of lifting those up at the bottom of society like His Holy Son did. The reputation of merchants is key to this endeavor. Swearing an oath to a particularly good merchant is not bad because, in order to be considered a good merchant one must have faith in them, and faith is the cornerstone of, well, the Faith.

We are saved by the faith we bestow in God. Faith is one of the only things God asks of us unconditionally. The effectiveness of His word can only be accounted for once faith is established.

It is no secret that I go so far as to suggest that all ledger pages should begin with the date followed by A.D., *anno domini*, in order to keep the name of God in the minds of businessmen all day long.

For it is upon taking account of one's business that a person can then determine the credits and debits owed to society as well. The ego of a businessman often consoles him into believing that his success in business is a direct result of his superior ability. To this determination, I do not argue. I do, however, point out that whatever superior ability exists belongs entirely to that which was bestowed by their Creator. And as a gift from God, it should be used to endow His other creatures with His divine power as well.

Therefore, if you are prosperous in your business dealings, you are endowed with riches not only for your own family, but to all your brothers and sisters. You must be generous with the resources that God has given you and fulfill objectives that decrease disparity between his creatures.

The dictum rings true. "Verily I say unto you, that a rich man shall hardly enter into the kingdom of heaven" (Matthew 19:23). In this way, being a proper Christian businessman, giving your vocation to God, and being generous to causes that increase the public good are practices that are not only good for business, since good Christians are sheltered from any such losses they might incur, but they are the only way to be saved from the hellfire of eternal damnation.

My *Summa* is not only a textbook for mathematics and a guidebook on double-entry bookkeeping, but a volley in the holy war for human souls.

There still loomed large one important question, though,

that would determine whether my *Summa* would actually accomplish the change I hoped for.

Would anyone buy it?

196,418

Chapter Twenty-Nine

THE RECEPTION

I didn't have to wait long to learn the answer. Soon, the consensus that the book was unique was touted this way: "No matter who you are, what you do, this book will help you, whereas most books do not." Of course, I disagreed vehemently with the last part of this statement, but I couldn't help but agree with its vigor.

In a world where instructional books were thriving, my book was a success. I couldn't have been happier. I think I smiled so much that new lines appeared around my eyes. At least, that's what I told myself since I was only slowly coming in account with my age. I was forty-eight, but felt a few years older.

My *Summa* was such a hit that the artist Jacopo de Barbari offered to paint my portrait. I was the first mathematician to have his portrait painted. I would have preferred that Leonardo paint it, but since he doesn't finish anything, had he started it, I probably would not have been the first. Piero had portraits of me in his tableaus, of course, but then again I was never the subject of those paintings, as I was now. To honor my memory of those days with Piero, I decided to have Guidobaldo pose in my portrait along with me. I did dedicate my *Summa* to him after all, and in that way I owed this success to him and all the students like him.

The book swept across Italy almost as fast as King Charles VIII of France invaded from the north. After Ludovico Sforza had overtaken the Duchy of Milan, he asked King Charles VIII to help him secure his position militarily and Charles obliged. As a fox invited into a henhouse, Charles didn't stop at bringing his troops to Milan and decided to conquer Italy all the way down to Naples as well.

While I was happy that my book, the greatest achievement of my life, was finally available to the public, I was sad that that public had to endure yet another war in the Italian peninsula. It reminded me of the Battle of the Stones from my youth. The war was brutal and pointless, a pissing ground for men who prided themselves on having muscles larger than their brains. To me, the invasion deepened the need for the book, to lift the minds of the populace and lean away from our more barbaric inclinations.

It was hard to be happy about it in the pure sense, but I was pleased when Ludovico Sforza, Venice, and Pope Alexander VI banded together, formed the League of Venice and tried to send King Charles VIII back to France.

The word was that they sent him packing without any spoils of war after the Battle of Fornovo. I knew what people meant, and the pride they felt saying it, but I couldn't help but ruminate on this simple fact: War is inherently spoiled. There is no treasure to be gained from it. Material possessions you seize in the enterprise only degrade the overall condition of your soul. There are no winners and losers. We all lose.

However, if I were compelled to crown one winner in the ordeal, and hopefully that time will never come, it would be Ludovico Sforza. While I disagreed with the events that led to his ability to do so, he had used his power play and the power that resulted from it to attract an exceptional court of artists, artisans, and engineers. Some of my colleagues referred to Ludovico's court in Milan as the New Athens, a remembrance of that city's position as a cradle of enlightened thinking, something we sorely needed more of.

Then, one day, I received a letter from Milan.

317,811

Chapter Thirty

THE NEW ATHENS

I was a magister, not just a university graduate, and a professor as well. I'd written and published books. Now, especially with my *Summa*, it was possible for me to be entertained in any court in Italy. But when the letter from Milan came, I swear, I did feel that it was out of step with my accomplishments.

Logic told me that the invitation was warranted, but the small-town boy that still lived in my brain, behind my years of toil and experience, told me that such an invitation was an error. Even so, I decided to answer it. It was an invitation to join the Sforza Court and I accepted it wholeheartedly.

The Sforza Court was the center of enlightenment thinking. It was populated by great men, including the inimitable chief architect Giovanni Antonio and his junior associate Donato Bramante who would later surpass him. (Perhaps Antonio was less inimitable than I initially thought.) There were the Sanseverino brothers, Galeazzo and Gaspare, both experts in military craft, which I despised but respected nonetheless. There were artists, artisans, and craftsmen of all stripes. There were stonemasons, weavers, metallurgists, painters, and sculptors, among them Giovanni Cristoforo Romano, a sculptor whose work I'd seen in the ducal palace in Urbino.

Another craftsman Ludovico had acquired for his court was Leonardo da Vinci. I didn't know much of the man on our first meeting, only that he had long been working on a horse sculpture or some such thing to honor Ludovico's father. From what I'd heard, though, it'd be Ludovico's grandchildren who would finally lay first eyes on the work's finished form, such was the slow progress on it.

Ludovico's welcome was warm, if not a bit ostentatious and grand. He assembled his court, filling an enormous hall with all the great men listed above and many more, all the intellectual spoils of a war that I disdained. Yet I could not help but revel in their glory. All these men were experts in their fields and I was about to become one of them, a part of this greater intellectual collective consciousness trying to push mankind forward, hopefully beyond the type of thinking that forged its creation.

I stood there, enraptured, as Ludovico sang my praises, calming my inner critic. He lauded my history with Alberti to Antonio and Bramante. He extolled my virtues to Romano, applauding my apprenticeship with Piero, another favorite artist of the duke.

Then he turned to Leonardo, lionizing my "natural talent in mathematics" as he called it, my many accomplishments, my degrees, my history as a cherished professor, and, of course, my *Summa*.

When Ludovico concluded, I thanked him profusely. "You don't know what it means to me to be welcomed into such an esteemed fraternity," I said. "I am humbled beyond measure, beyond words. You are definitely a court *sui generis*."

I had, as you may know, finished my regards in Latin, saying they were "of their own kind," trying to compliment them as much as they had me. Although now with the advantage of time, I think they were present at my arrival more to appease their patron than yours truly. While I had no ill will in my remark, apparently not all parties felt my humble gratitude.

"Not all of us speak Latin," Leonardo said curtly.

"I'm sorry," I apologized. "It means that . . ."

"I know what it means," Leonardo interrupted. "I didn't learn it in a book, though. Artists need to have natural talent, something you can't learn through sheer application like a mathematician." He finished this sentence with a sneer, cementing its negative intent.

Bastard! I thought. It was only later that I learned Leonardo actually was one, having been born out of wedlock to a father who wouldn't recognize him as his own. He could have been legitimized, and I'm still to this day not quite sure why he wasn't. His father, Ser Piero da Vinci, was a notary and could have made Leonardo his legitimate son easily with the Gonfaloniere of Florence. He didn't need a papal letter as the two illegitimate Malatesta sons had done.

But if what I encountered that day was any indication of his demeanor as a child, I can, although perhaps I shouldn't, say that I understood why his father didn't want official recognition that Leonardo was his son. While Leonardo was only seven years younger than I was, his maturity, at times, even at his now advanced age, seemed more in line with that of an impudent child than a grown man. Perhaps my foray into Latin set him off. I would later learn he was denied a formal education, one that would have included Latin. Or perhaps it was my position in life that led him to be so brusque—by then I was a magister, a professor, and a friar, a man of esteemed position not beholden to any earthly man. Leonardo, on the other hand, was a painter and an engineer, a craftsman, and his work depended on him having a patron.

In that moment, though, I didn't care what Leonardo's reasons were for acting this way. It took all my strength to restrain the hot-blooded boy in my brain. I'm sure I smiled politely, demurely, at Leonardo's barb, but I felt more inclined to bare my teeth like an animal, and gnaw and gnash at his flesh until he relented. What had I done to justify such a discourtesy?

Everything I had worked for in my life had brought me to this moment. I was now a member of a court that consisted of both my idols and my peers. I had earned my spot here through hard work and diligence, and here was this man-child trying to make my first impression with this esteemed court my last.

But I swallowed my consternation, restrained my rage, and replied to Leonardo calmly.

"You're right," I said. "If it were not for the many years I've spent applying myself to my craft and the graciousness of mentors who lifted me out of ignorance, I would not be here today."

This caused something in Leonardo's demeanor to shift. Perhaps it was my own graciousness toward him, but his eyes hinted a level of respect I had not yet seen in his penetrating, seemingly unrelenting gaze. Despite noticing this shift, however, his next words still surprised me.

"No," Leonardo said. "You wouldn't be here unless I had Ludovico invite you."

514,229

Chapter Thirty-One

THE FIRST SUPPER

That night, we dined. I thought I had become numb to fancy feasts, having dined with dukes and popes, but I learned that the meals that Ludovico Sforza managed to concoct were nothing short of miraculous. This was due, in no small part, to the intricate pageants Leonardo da Vinci would stage, dazzling and delighting the assembled denizens with a mixture of theatrics and technical wizardry I never thought possible. I'd love to go into more depth, recounting the specific details of these magnificent productions and the wonder they elicited deep in my soul, but I fear that doing so would undercut the magical effects and utter delight they were able to cause in all who were lucky enough to experience them.

The ephemeral quality of Leonardo's pageants contributed to their beauty, but Leonardo, as I soon would learn, wanted to contribute something more eternal to the canon of history, something more substantial than a master of ceremonies was allowed to create. He wanted to be known as a great painter.

That night, I learned many things. Indeed, it had been

Leonardo himself who, having apparently been enamored of my *Summa*, had requested, nay beseeched, Ludovico to secure my services. This fact, contrasted with his treatment of me upon my arrival, still confounds me to this day, despite now having spent enough time with the man to be fully inculcated with his, let me be courteous and say, divergent personality.

Leonardo was working on the underdrawing of a new painting in the Santa Maria della Grazie and he needed my help. Unlike Botticelli, Leonardo wanted to incorporate correct perspective in his mural, and I, being the preeminent academic in visual perspective, and having studied directly with the two late masters of the field, was the man that Leonardo wanted to talk to. As I would learn, Leonardo was a man with capabilities beyond the definition of brilliant, but he would seek out the advice of others if they had greater knowledge in an area than he possessed. Those who knew him would corroborate that this was rarely the case, though.

I also learned that Donato Bramante had pounded the same streets in Urbino at precisely the same time I had frequented them, although it was not until that very night our paths finally crossed.

And I learned never to cross Caterina Sforza, Ludovico's niece. She asked Gaspare, half of the pair of Sanseverino brothers I mentioned, and the more handsome one at that, to dance. When he declined, saying that dancing and music was none of his business, being a man of war and little else, as was so often the case, Caterina pounced on his reluctance.

"Since you're not at war," she countered, "you should request to be well-oiled and locked away in a cupboard to avoid becoming any rustier than you already are."

832,040

Chapter Thirty-Two

THE LAST SUPPER

I stood in the future burial chamber of Ludovico Sforza, a grand mausoleum in the Santa Maria della Grazie that Sforza was renovating in his own honor. A new painting by Leonardo da Vinci took up a whole wall, or at least, the underdrawing for a painting did. It was to be of the Lord, our Jesus Christ, and his apostles at the Last Supper. Leonardo was already a year into the commission, but hadn't progressed past the underdrawing, which is why he summoned me.

Leonardo had incorporated many of the rudimentary aspects of perspective in his underdrawing. It was clear he knew how to use a plummet line and compass, but as soon as I saw the painting I knew something was off, albeit ever so slightly.

"The perspective is perfect. It's just not perfect from everyone's perspective," lamented Leonardo.

I knew what he meant. Leonardo had attempted to align the lines of the mausoleum ceiling with those in his underdrawing, visually extending the mausoleum into the world of his painting, far beyond the physical wall it was drawn upon. But unless the viewer was situated precisely at the spot in the room where the illusion would manifest, the imparted illusion would be that of disillusion.

"It would have been a clever trick if God had not made men of all different heights and given them legs to walk around and distort the effect further," I consoled.

But Leonardo was never one to take consolation as an accolade.

"I thought you'd be able to tell me something I didn't know, some scientific trick outside the bounds of your tome to calculate a median or some optimum perspective regardless of these earthly differences," he said.

"Unfortunately, I put all my knowledge inside the book and carry no private tricks for myself," I apologized.

I saw the look of disappointment on Leonardo's face. It was the same look of pained anger and resignation you'd see on the face of a child after you dangled a sweet over his head and then withdrew it before the he could grasp it, not that I would have any experience with that. Luckily, I thought of an idea that might cheer Leonardo up.

"Perhaps, since the problem is earthly," I responded. "The solution should be Heavenly. Instead of calculating the perspective from the individual and ever-changing point of view of man, perhaps the perspective should emanate from the ever-constant and omnipotent view of God and that of his embodiment in this painting, Jesus Christ. Since all things come from God, the perspective could be from that of Christ, radiating out like the Son he is."

At first, Leonardo didn't seem particularly happy with this

solution. A few of his breaths hitched and he seemed like he was hit with a sudden bout of nausea.

"It may not be entirely logical," he uttered. "But it may be the best solution nonetheless, given the circumstances."

Then Leonardo's face brightened and he said, "It would put the horizon at the median, though, which wouldn't be horrible."

If the release of tension in my body were any guide, it was this moment when the tension between Leonardo and I finally started to abate, and the friendship between us started to grow.

I need hardly remind you, as you've surely seen many copies of it, that Leonardo quickly put his pupils to work, changing the perspective of his work to come from Him.

The only person seemingly more perturbed by the change of course was the head of the monastery at the Santa Maria della Grazie, who, after learning that Leonardo and his pupils were redoing the underdrawing from scratch, stormed into the mausoleum and screeched his disapproval.

"You can't start over!" he sputtered as he bounded in. "You've only just started and it's already been a year!"

"Finally, I've found the face of Judas!" Leonardo spat. "Hobble back to your lair or I swear your face will forever be enshrined as that of His executioner! Then see if St. Peter lets you in."

The friar's head fell fast. In all my years in the Church, I've never seen the fear of the Lord inspired in someone so quickly. Please don't write this down, but his name was . . . and I wouldn't be surprised if he needed a change of clothes after that dressing down. The man sighed, took small steps on his way out, and murmured in a monotone over his shoulder, "Please let me know if you require anything. I am at your service."

Perhaps I was curious to see if there would be any more

dramatics, but I stayed to supervise the new perspective grid for the underdrawing, making sure Leonardo's pupils had learned the lessons of the plummet line and compass that were handed down to me from Piero della Francesca, and that Leonardo had already taught himself.

When the perspective grid was complete, I lingered, watching Leonardo continue his work. I gawked as he brought in locals from the crowds and markets in Milan to serve as models for the apostles. He told me the number of faces was finite, only so many combinations of noses and brows and mouths that he could use for his painting. He said he already had all these combinations in his head, but they cycled endlessly upon each other, drowning the decisions he needed to make in a sea of possibilities. Fishing for faces in crowds and markets narrowed his options, but he said he always reeled in the finest possible choice.

Leonardo brought in a particularly degenerate gentleman for Judas Iscariot. Although the head of the monastery wasn't particularly pleased to have a man of his character there, he was relieved that the man was taking his place in Leonardo's personification of the character nonetheless. The man was seemingly already on a course to damnation so Leonardo thought he wasn't doing any more harm by binding him with the image of Judas than he had already brought upon himself.

Although Leonardo didn't seem initially exuberant to recalculate his work from Christ's perspective, I caught him slotting in references to the Holy Trinity. He drew Christ, His arms extending outward down to the table creating an equilateral triangle, each side being equal and one-third of the whole. There were three windows along the back wall. And all the apostles were posing in groups of three. To Jesus's right sat Judas, Peter, and John together and then Bartholomew, James, son of Alphaeus, and Andrew. To the left of Jesus were Thomas, James the Greater, and Philip in one tableau and then Matthew, Thadeus, and Simon in another. These were all markers of the Trinitarian mystery, the essential nature of divinity in three persons.

I scrutinized the details he added to the underdrawing. And that's when I saw it. In details large and small, Leonardo was doing something, well, divine.

1,346,269

Chapter Thirty-Three

DIVINE INSPIRATION

"One of you will betray me," Jesus spoke to the apostles, although the phrase could have easily slipped from Leonardo's lips. He always seemed at odds with one pupil or another, or perhaps one demon or another. He often sat and stared at the painting for a long period of time, not working, just staring, as if contemplating the next brush stroke.

As fraught as his thinking must have been, the painting he was executing was even more complex. It was intricate. And glorious. Deliberately and diligently, he was incorporating the divine proportion in his work. I saw it all over the design of the painting. It was in the height of Jesus and the apostles compared to the height of the ceiling. It was in the relationship between the top of the table to the top of the window, which could then be compared to the top of the window to the top of the ceiling. It was in the height of the table in relation to the height of the ceiling. It was the height of the window in relation to the height of the ceiling. It was the width of the center window to the width of the ceiling. It was the distance between Jesus and John to His right. It was in the ornamental shields above *The Last Supper*, in the width of the shields compared to the width of their alcoves. It was all over the place. And it was in the smallest details, even defining the relationship between the heights of the two layers of molding separating the ceiling from the shields. Everywhere my eye wandered, I could see it. The very same ratio that Euclid had first defined in his thirteenth book of the *Elements*, the book that was written in Greek, which was as foreign to Leonardo's ear as Latin or a father's love.

"How did you do it?" I questioned Leonardo with the same incredulity one might ask a particularly charmed soothsayer. I hadn't touched on the divine proportion in my *Summa*.

"Euclid's diagrams need no translation," Leonardo responded flatly.

This was, at least in Leonardo's case, true. Unlike Vitruvius, Euclid had provided diagrams of his teachings and Leonardo had, a bit miraculously, although he might not believe in that concept, intuited the concept of the divine proportion without knowledge of the language describing the diagrams. And here Leonardo was using those divine proportions systematically, or one could say, religiously, that is, if Leonardo's biblical inclinations were less known to me.

I was surprised and delighted. As far as I knew, he was the first painter to incorporate the divine proportion in his work. Even Piero, my dear mentor and authority on all things painting and perspective, never incorporated the proportion into his work, but then again, Piero was never the perennial student that Leonardo was, always seeking out answers to questions far afield than those of his official capacity. Since Leonardo was denied a classical education, he used the world around him as a classroom.

He was a man truly at the forefront of our time, seemingly a master or skilled apprentice in all trades.

Leonardo said that he was using the ratio in his painting, because, like the ancient mathematicians before us, he was fascinated by it.

"It's a ratio of proportion that pops up frequently in nature. It lives in leaves and branches and along the stems of plants. And it's in the veins of the leaves. It's in veins of humans and in the bodies of animals. It's everywhere. It's a consistent pattern, a unifying principle. A scientific order to the universe," he extolled. "And since my painting practice represents all that I can see and know, incorporating the proportion is not solely an obsession, but a requirement of my work."

"I couldn't agree more," I concurred. "The divine proportion is a sign of His divine plan connecting all of His creation. It's the marker of the harmonic relation between the whole and the part, intricately complimenting each other as do the Father, Son, and the Holy Spirit. It's the most cogent and consistent proof of His existence."

I finished this last sentence almost breathlessly. I was so full of emotion, the euphoria of the moment completely engulfing all sensation in my body. I felt like I was radiating warmth, as if I had just come out of a hot bath. I was so happy to have found my counterpart in Leonardo, someone so in tune with what I saw as the mystery and wonder of the universe. It was these emotions, this excitement and hope, that made his next statement all the more disheartening.

"I don't believe in God," Leonardo said in a dull monotone.

Judas! I thought. What I had intuited before, but left willfully unprocessed, was that Leonardo might not be on the same side as I was on when it came to certain issues.

"I'm an atheist," he rejoined, digging the knife he'd lodged in my heart even deeper.

We eyed each other for a long moment, sizing each other up, trying to determine where we wanted this discussion to go next, each of us simultaneously intrigued and repulsed by the other's ideological guidance. Leonardo broke the silence.

"Would you like to work with me to uncover its secrets anyway?" he proposed.

I'd like to think that this was a test from God because if it was then I passed with flying colors. But if it wasn't, I knew a certain man three places to the right of Jesus who might have an easier time getting past St. Peter than I. While we disagreed on the higher purpose and origin of the divine proportion, Leonardo and I were both clearly fascinated by it. We made an odd couple, surely, one atheist and one devout friar, but I could see in his eyes that although he wasn't a believer in God, Leonardo was a strict devotee of intellectual curiosity, spiritual in his own way.

While the mystery of His way in still unclear to me to this day, what was clear to me at the time was that if I ever had a chance to uncover the divine proportion's secrets, Leonardo was the man to partner with to do so.

"When do we start?"

2,178,309

Chapter Thirty-Four

THE IRRATIONAL COLLABORATION

"First, we shall talk of the proportions of man. Because from the human body derive all measures and their denominations. And in it is to be found all and every ratio and proportion by which God reveals the innermost secrets of nature," I blurted out at the beginning of our first meeting, perhaps more of a test than an initiation. I had to make it clear to him that I would be an equal member of our collaboration, lest his instinct to treat me like one of his pupils became too strong.

Leonardo was more than happy to oblige. The ancient philosopher Vitruvius had laid down the premise that the human body fits inside both a circle and a square, but he didn't leave drawings to explain his conclusion. Every artist who came after him, including Francesco di Giorgio, Cesare Cesariano, and Fra. Giocondo, had tried to circle the square and failed. They had taken Vitruvius at his word, produced drawings and sculptures that fit Vitruvius' description. But their works had hands and feet larger than an actual human's, which therefore, in some people's eyes, negated the dictum.

Even Michelangelo in creating his giant sculpture of David, didn't get the proportions right. David's hands and feet are much too large, far out of proportion with the natural male body. Some of Michelangelo's devotees tried to convince me that the proportion was off because it was originally meant to be displayed on the roof of the Duomo (as if a work that large could ever be supported by the roof), that Michelangelo meant for the hands and feet to be larger so that, from the angle below, each body part would appear to be in correct proportion. To the uninitiated, this might explain Michelangelo's folly, but it is grossly ignorant of how perspective actually works.

So, I'd have to politely educate them—since I was the direct intellectual descendant of the man who invented linear algebra and thus perspective, Brunelleschi—that if an artist wanted a sculpture's hands and feet to seem proportionate when viewed from below, he would make them smaller than the limbs above because they would be closer. So, by making the hands and feet larger, he actually exacerbated the problem by doing the exact opposite of what correct perspective demands.

But I'm getting ahead of myself. At this point, Michelangelo had not yet started his David. So please, when I get to the point where I mention the Giant, please know that this is the ill-conceived work I'm talking about.

Leonardo was convinced that Vitruvius was correct, though, and that these artists were misinterpreting his statement. The only complication in his conviction was that he didn't understand what Vitruvius meant either. We were both sure, however, that the divine proportion had a hand in uncovering it. Vitruvius had somehow proportioned the perfect circle and the perfect square in relation to the correct positioning of the human form. A human was supposed to be able to fit into both. The solution would surely be obvious once it was found, if only it ever were.

Unfortunately, it didn't seem like we would be the ones to unearth it. We didn't make much progress. We connected the square to the edges of a circle as others had done. We spent days going over how it could be done differently, during the hours Leonardo was not painting *The Last Supper*. We constantly speculated on the solution to Vitruvius's mystery, hoping that it would unlock the greater mystery of His ratio and His way. The universe was surely created with mathematical models, a geometry of divine perfection. If we could unlock it we could unlock the whole of human knowledge, at least in theory. It could be a *reductio in unitatum*, a reduction toward unity, although I hesitated saying anything like that around Leonardo, at least in Latin.

As Leonardo's work, *The Last Supper*, took form, our collaboration fell flat, producing no solid way forward toward Vitruvius's solution.

Dispirited by our initial failure together, but still spurred by the intellectual spirit, we decided to switch gears and work on something else, hoping that the time away would awaken another path forward.

Perhaps our collaboration was as doomed as *The Last Supper*. Almost as soon as he finished the painting in February of the year of the Lord 1498, Leonardo's work of art began to perish. During one of our sessions, one in which I may have let slip my consultation with Botticelli, Leonardo had declared that, "Botticelli's paintings are old-fashioned as soon as he puts paint to canvas. Soon to be relics of history. This one will not be."

To that end, Leonardo had not only sought to create the

correct depth and perspective in his painting, which Botticelli had stubbornly refused to do, but he had also concocted an ingenious method to enhance the brightness of the paint using an undercoat of white lead. It was a clever innovation, but unfortunately one that led to his downfall, since the undercoat, having only been invented for the work it was gracing, had therefore not been thoroughly tested and caused the plaster to chip away and decay in some sections, almost even before the last stroke of his brush had left its surface. It was decomposing so quickly that, unlike Botticelli's paintings, history might not even have the opportunity to mark Leonardo's new work.

All was for naught anyway, for reasons that I'm sure you're more than familiar with. Perhaps it was God's retribution for Leonardo's disbelief, or for his insistence that the apostles did not have halos, as was their right and the broader custom. For whatever reason, for Ludovico's sins or for Leonardo's, *The Last Supper* was not meant to grace Ludovico Sforza's grand mausoleum. After Ludovico's fall from grace, it became a place where friars said theirs. The grand Sforza mausoleum became a refectory, a dining hall for the friars at the monastery.

3,524,578

Chapter Thirty-Five

THE HORSE

The other project Leonardo and I would frequently spend our time contemplating, in between bouts of inspiration and frustration, was his infamous horse. As I mentioned, the horse was meant to be a great tribute to Ludovico's father. Or was it Ludovico himself? Perhaps both. Either way, it was going to be the largest statue made of bronze in the world and Leonardo was going to have two crowning achievements during his tenure in Milan, if he could ever figure out how to make the pour work, that is.

Yes, as you may know, the techniques for pouring bronze statues had long ago been invented, but Leonardo's horse was going to be on a scale not yet seen. The apparatus for achieving such a pour simply did not exist, yet this fact did not dissuade Leonardo from his pursuit. Rather it was an inspiration, a technical challenge to be overcome that was, in some ways, more exciting for Leonardo to achieve than the actual statue. I helped him calculate the amount of bronze he'd need to fill the mold as Leonardo was busy drawing. He needed to invent and then build the apparatus that would birth his creation. Everything was going relatively well on this quest, a clear contrast to the failure we experienced trying to step into Vitruvius's footprints, until the very moment we had everything lined up and all that we had to do was execute Leonardo's vision.

The apparatus was built, the amount of bronze calculated, the artisans ready. But suddenly, there was no bronze. All the bronze that had been set aside for Leonardo's horse had been used to make cannons for war instead.

Leonardo apparently accosted the duke, Ludovico that is. I heard he threw the last remaining brick of bronze at Ludovico's head in front of his war ministers, almost creating a war himself. As much as I abhor violence, I would have liked to have seen that.

Leonardo didn't stay mad for long, though, or at least he didn't have much of an opportunity to do so because the French invaded Milan. The cannons that Ludovico made did not thwart their attack. Even if Leonardo had been able to pour his horse, the French would have melted it down to contribute to their own offenses anyway.

"I wasn't angry at Ludovico because he took away my horse," Leonardo would later tell me. "I had already made the horse in my head. I had already solved the puzzle. I was angry at him because he took away my chance for others to be amazed at it. He took away my chance to have a great achievement that others can hold in their minds for generations to come. He took away my chance to be remembered."

5,702,887

Chapter Thirty-Six

THE ESCAPE

Leonardo and his slender, curly haired assistant, Salai, picked me up in a horse cart on the outskirts of the city. We had all just escaped the castle as the flaming French arrows fell upon the castle.

King Charles VIII of France died and his successor, Louis XII, wanted to reestablish France's claim over Milan, however tenuous it really was. As was so often the case, one man's death begat the death of many others.

We rode away from a city in flames, a city where Leonardo left his life's greatest works unfinished or fading, a city that may just as well have burned up my hopes and dreams along with it, a city that beckoned me with its siren song, albeit a short sweet song with a scornful finale.

We all had dark circles under our eyes, or was it ash from the fire? Leonardo and I left Milan depressed, having attained none of the great achievements we had set out for ourselves. I lay in the back of the horse cart in place of my bed, watching the scenery pass by as the finality of this moment set in.

Perhaps it was Salai, or perhaps it was a lack of other options, but we decided to flee to Mantua. Francesco and Isabella d'Este, the Marquis and Marchesa respectively, welcomed us with open arms. The question of why Mantua was on the short list for we dear refugees became apparent soon upon our arrival.

"Leonardo!" Isabella beckoned. "I've heard the news from Milan and I couldn't be happier. You finally have time to do my portrait!"

9,227,465

Chapter Thirty-Seven

BEGONE DULL CARE

We needed to figure out our next move. So, naturally, we played chess. Leonardo and I languished in long, lazy afternoons spent simmering in this sport of strained suspense. This helped my attitude and outlook improve considerably, since my mind was suspended in the anxiety of this trivial pursuit, and not in my anxiety about our lack of prospects.

If I had to hazard a guess, and I were a betting man, I would bet that our draw rate was around seventy percent. So, more often than not, there would be no victor in our battle of wits and "bits," the name Leonardo would give to any number of pieces, frequently goading me with a "If you move that bit this bit will . . ." and so on and so forth.

They weren't called bits, though, of course. There were the pawns, the knights, the elephants, the rooks, the vizier to counsel the king, and of course, the king himself. Our hostess Isabella soon amended us of a few of these pieces. She found out about our chess games and quickly produced herself at one of our matches along with a most resplendent set of chessmen made by none other than the Milanese craftsman Cleofas Donati.

"So, are you playing by the old rules or the new rules?" Isabella asked, presenting us an appeal too appealing to expel.

"I did not know the rules were in need of revision," Leonardo responded.

"Pray tell, what are these new rules you speak of?" I asked, applying more allure than my associate.

Isabella plunked herself down next to us and pronounced, "It's called Queen's Chess."

"The new rules are," she said, starting to show us on the board in front of her as well as in our mind's eye, "that pawns can move forward two squares on their first move, instead of one. Elephants are now called bishops, and instead of only being able to jump two spaces diagonally, they can move forward diagonally as far as you like as long as the path is clear."

"I thought this was called Queen's Chess," Leonardo interrupted.

"Which brings me to the last and most important change," Isabella continued, her eyes narrowing a bit. "The vizier is now a queen. And she's powerful. The vizier can only move one space diagonally, but the queen can move in any direction, as far as she wants, as long as her path is clear of any annoying pawns," she said, perhaps glancing at Leonardo a bit too meaningfully.

"What if it's a knight?" Leonardo asked, placing a knight in the path of the queen on the board.

"More often than not, it's a pawn. But even when it's a knight, or any other piece, she needs a clear line of sight to advance. If she doesn't have a clear line of sight, though, she can make her own," Isabella said, punctuating this line by knocking down the knight with her queen.

"Want to play?" she asked, although it was more of a challenge since she stared right at Leonardo.

"I'd be delighted," Leonardo responded.

"Would you like me list the rules again?" she asked.

"It's not necessary," said Leonardo.

"What are we playing for?" Isabella inquired.

"What do I have that you're lacking?" Leonardo probed.

"All these days spent playing chess, you could have been working on my painting. If I win, if I best you, you'll do it. You'll paint my portrait," Isabella said.

"And if I win I . . ."

"If you win," Isabella interrupted, "you can continue spending your afternoons on my grounds unmolested by my reasonable requests."

Leonardo nodded his consent.

"Ladies first," Leonardo offered.

"No, please, after you," Isabella rejoined. "I'm no lady, after all. I'm a Marchesa."

And with that, Leonardo moved his first pawn forward two squares, the one in front of his king.

"You've exposed your king," Isabella uttered.

"I'm not afraid to . . ."

Isabella moved the pawn in front of her king two spaces forward as well, silencing him, and seemingly taking his bait.

Then Leonardo, smiling, moved out his right knight in front of his right bishop.

Isabella, smiling even wider, moved her queen diagonally all the way to the edge of the board.

"It's too bad she can't do anything from there," Leonardo goaded, before moving his knight forward and setting it down right next to her pawn.

"It's too bad your knight can't do anything from way out there either," Isabella riposted before moving the bishop to the right of her king four spaces, placing it right next to Leonardo's knight.

"Well, how about I get a bit closer then," Leonardo said as he moved his knight directly in front of her king.

"Oh, that sounds nice," Isabella said as she advanced her queen, taking the pawn in front of the bishop to the left of Leonardo's king.

"Isn't the queen supposed to be powerful in this game?" Leonardo chided as he started his king toward Isabella's queen. "And yet you sacrificed . . ."

"I don't think you can do that," Isabella interrupted, stopping Leonardo in his tracks. "No, I'm sorry. I know you can't do that. That's checkmate."

Leonardo sat there, stupefied, as Isabella pointed out the bishop guarding the queen's current position.

"She just waited for the right moment to pounce," Isabella explained.

Indeed, she had.

"Well, that was quick," I said, trying to ease the tension between them, but in retrospect, only adding to it.

"They describe this style as '*a la rabiosa*,'" she said. "For the rabid."

Isabella was quite a skillful player, frequently besting both of us, sometimes even playing both Leonardo and me at the same time. For all her ability on the chess board, though, she was never able to get Leonardo to paint her portrait, despite their wager. Leonardo did produce a drawing of her, but stalled on the painting. If Leonardo's heart, or more precisely his mind, was not in it, then it was nearly impossible to get him to take on a new task.

He told her he intended to paint her, though, all the while saying to me in confidence that he was only doing so to advance the availability of our accommodations, until such time as we figured out where to go next. We hadn't yet uncovered the secrets of the divine proportion and were keen on working together until we had, in between bouts of this new, more exciting version of chess, that is.

Perhaps Isabella sensed our restlessness or Leonardo's willingness to let her portrait remain unfinished, because she proposed that I write a book about chess. It was a cunning move. She knew my penchant for books, sensing I'd jump at the chance to write another, especially if she sponsored my work as she promised to do. I wholeheartedly accepted the commission, the diversion of writing of a book about a diversion seemed too delicious to desert.

The history of chess was an interesting one. It had emerged from Hindustan or Persia or one of the Arab lands 1,000 years before. And although it was new to us, the queen had made her first appearance about 500 years before, but she was then not the powerhouse she was now. At first, she could only move one space at a time, and then, only diagonally. They called chess *chaturanga* in Sanskrit, or "four members," meaning the four parts of the Hindustani army: the elephants, and chariots, and cavalry, and infantry. Does everything have to be based on war? But I digress. Chess, like mathematics, has a great debt to the Arab world. The design of the pieces follows the Islamic tradition of abstracting God's creations. Even the term *checkmate*, as uttered so thrillingly from Isabella's lips, came from the Persian *shah mat*, which translates as "the king is flummoxed."

Perhaps to balance this debt with a credit, Isabella I of Castile, the ruler of Spain along with her husband Ferdinand, the same two monarchs who have been sending that Columbus fellow back and forth along the new passage to Asia, had been taking the game of chess and embarking it on a new journey of its own. Perhaps they were inspired by a poem called "Love Chess" which recited a game played with the new rules as if it were a love story. Regardless of whether or not they were inspired by this poem, the Spanish Isabella did fall in love with the game. She commissioned not one, but two books on the subject. *Libre dels jochs partites dels schacs en nombre de 100 (The book of 100 chess problems)* which was published in Valencia a few years ago in 1495, written by Francesch Vicent, I should mention. And *Repetición de amores e arte de axedres con CL iuegos de partido (Discourse on love and the art of chess with 150 problems)*, written by Luis Ramíriz de Lucena, and published in Salamanca a year or so later.

It was he who coined the title "Queen's Chess" and it was in the vein of these books that my Isabella, Isabella d'Este, wanted me to write my new commission. But written in Italian, of course, for her subjects since they couldn't read these tomes written in Catalan and Spanish, the ones I just listed.

Thinking of those lazy, aimless days in Mantua, I couldn't help but call this new work *Schifanoia* or "Begone Dull Care." Although *De ludo scachorum (On the Game of Chess)* was a more appropriate title, and when it finally went to printing, I went with that title instead.

To me, writing another book was a logical step. I wanted to get knowledge, both mine and that which I had accumulated from those around me, out into the world. I am, more than anything else, a teacher. I want to educate people. Leonardo and I were an odd couple in so many ways. He the traditionally unschooled, gruff but brilliant atheist, and me, the magister and man of God and manners, in that order. But it was in this respect that we were perhaps the most different. Where I felt an inherent compulsion to educate those who came after me, Leonardo felt no such desire. Nevertheless I couldn't help but goad him in that direction, continually asking, "You write all day in your notebooks. Why don't you publish any of your work?"

It is perhaps the one area of difference between us that time and conversation seems not able to bridge. But since we get along so well in so many other areas I decided to not press this matter upon him too greatly with the hope that he would come to his senses in due time.

14,930,352

Chapter Thirty-Eight

THE NEXT MOVE

Back to the Flower. Together, we decided to go back to Florence, the city of my magister and Leonardo's apprenticeship. Although I am a Franciscan friar and it is a Servite order church, I was able to arrange accommodations in the cloisters of the Santissima Annunziata Church due to my relative fraternity and level of fame and reputation. It's nice to have brothers wherever you may go.

Leonardo planned to stay with his family in town, but apparently that didn't work out because he came to the Santissima Annunziata practically begging for accommodation. I was only able to secure him a stay there on the promise that he would provide services to the church. My sin in this venture was great. I knew Leonardo never intended to work for them, even if they commissioned him a work, but I felt the opportunity to continue working together, or at least be near each other hoping for the possibility of a breakthrough, outweighed the potential

Heavenly costs. Leonardo and his assistant Salai took up living quarters next to mine.

It was then that I started seeing why Leonardo would never pass on his knowledge in a book. He moved too fast from one thing to another. For instance, upon our arrival to Florence, he became preoccupied with getting a commission for a sculpture made out of a slab of marble that everyone called the Giant. And then, the next moment, he let loose of that goal, or perhaps the choice to let go of it was not his, and he was painting a portrait of some local merchant's wife. Why would he choose to paint this woman instead of Isabella d'Este? I heard it wasn't even a proper commission, that he was not receiving any money for it. Leonardo skipped around too quickly, from one project to another, never finishing any of them.

So, determined that our collaboration would not befall the same fate as his individual artistic projects, I set out to standardize and quantify our interactions in the best way I knew how, by outlining and executing a new book. It would be about the divine proportion, although maybe not exclusively dedicated to it, but definitely inspired by it, called *De divina proportione* (*On divine proportion*). In a perhaps more rhetorical flourish, due to the importance of the knowledge therein, I gave it the full title of *On divine proportion: a work for all perspicacious and curious intellects, necessary for all who study philosophy, perspective, painting, sculpture, architecture, music, and other mathematics arts. A pleasing, subtle, and admirable doctrine follows and delights with various questions of secret knowledge.*

It was a book to be born out of the intellectually engrossing scientific debates Leonardo and I had in Milan and those between the esteemed members of the New Athens, sometimes in the presence of Ludovico himself. The goal was to support a bedrock for this now secret scientific knowledge, providing a potent and wonderful doctrine for others to learn and follow.

To that end, I tried to focus Leonardo's attention away from his artistic endeavors and onto mathematics. In this regard, I succeeded handsomely, supplying elaborate geometrical puzzles for us to solve and discovering together, with my knowledge of perspective and his gift for drawing, how to create the effect of multi-faceted, three-dimensional regular bodies on a sheet of paper. I was so effective in this pursuit that Leonardo would often say that he couldn't even "bear the brush," preferring our endeavors to his artistic ones.

We continued on in this way for approximately four years. Ultimately, my *Divina* featured three sections: the *Compendio de divina proportione* (*Compendium of divine proportion*), the *Tractato del' architectura* (*Treatise on architecture*), and the *Libellus in tres partiales tractatus divisus quinque corporum regularium et dependentium* (*Treatise on the five regular bodies*). Apart from these three sections, but still part of the whole, I included a section on the roman capital letters that I drew with a straight edge and compass and another section on the regular solids drawn by Leonardo's hand, although this latter section came later. So, in this way, you could say that the book has five sections.

The *Compendio*, the first section, starts with a summary and a list of properties of the divine proportion, as one might expect. I also discuss the various Plantonic solids and other polyhedra, but the most important part of this section (important enough at least for me to recite below, as I am about to do, perhaps the only time that I will do so in this book, since my other books are generally much better sources to learn about the actual concepts I'm discussing here), is in the fifth chapter, where I describe the Holy divinity of the numbers I put forth in the books and explain why they should remain known as the divine proportion. It perhaps need not be said, though, that I often tried to shield Leonardo from this explanation and intention.

But first, for those uninitiated, I'll offer a basic explanation of how the divine proportion is calculated. If you are already educated in this, please feel to skip ahead to the numbered section below.

The divine proportion is the number which is achieved by dividing a line into two parts in a manner which, when you divide the length of the longer part by the length of the smaller part, is equal to the length of both parts divided by the length of the longer part.

If you are lost, don't be. Please use the formula below to better illuminate this relationship, this proportion between segments.

The divine proportion can be achieved thusly, when: $a/b = (a+b)/a$

As long as the proportion is correct, it will always produce the number 1.61803398874989484820458683436563811772 03091798 . . . and so on and so forth, continuing on into infinity, as does His Lord our creator.

So here, to you my dear reader, and my trusty penman, I lay out these reasons why the proportion described in further detail in my *Divina* is divine:

1. There is only one God. And there is only one Divine Proportion.

2. As there is the Father, Son, and the Holy Spirit, the divine proportion also contains three quantities within itself.

3. The divine proportion cannot be thoroughly represented by any rational quantity, just as God cannot be thoroughly understood or defined with words, His true magnificence lying beyond our limited comprehension. The divine proportion, having no rational quantity, will remained concealed and secret, as too does the true nature of God.

4. The divine proportion does not shrink or waver. It is everywhere and does not change. It is in things both large and small. In this regard, the relationship to God is clear and does not need further explanation on this point.

5. There are five elements: Earth, water, air, fire and Heavenly virtue, the last of which created the other four and the divine proportion contained within them. In return, and this I include from Plato's Timaeus, we create the form of Heaven in the dodecahedron, the regular body whose twelve faces are pentagons, each possessing diagonals in divine proportion to its sides.

I talk more about these regular, multi-faceted bodies in the third section, although they are also be discussed in the second one on architecture as well. Perhaps I was thinking about my old mentor Alberti, but I decided that I would include a section on architecture in the book as well. It was a little further afield than I was used to writing about, but it was fascinating nonetheless. For instance, the rhombicuboctahedron can be seen as either an expanded cube or an expanded octahedron. Leonardo loved that one. And I was able to show how the twenty-six-sided rhombicuboctahedron and its stellated truncated form with seventy-two sides were used in the construction of the Pantheon in Rome.

Although it was built 1,400 years prior, the Pantheon is still larger than Il Duomo in Florence, with its magnificent dome designed by Brunelleschi, Alberti's mentor and, by proxy, mine. Although I had mostly given up on the attempt, this was yet another example I used to prod Leonardo into passing on his knowledge, should his techniques be lost as were those used in the construction of the Pantheon.

Unfortunately, when he wasn't in our workshop, Leonardo was occupied with other adventures, including trying to, and I say this plainly, devise a machine that would let him fly like a bird. While I applauded his efforts, I more often had to help patch his wounds, when his assistant Salai wasn't there, since these endeavors led to more broken bones than results.

I had outside engagements as well, though. I was hired to teach both at the University of Florence and the University of Pisa. It was two assignments, although the schools were partially combined, in geography as much as educational philosophy. I lauded these schools. They were public, to the extent that no tuition was charged to any of the students. They were institutions to advance the public good as was the school of my youth and I became the principal drummer extolling their virtues. It is for this reason that I gave Piero Soderini, the Gonfaloniere of Florence, responsible for administering all aspects of the city, one of the first copies of my *Divina* upon its completion. I would not finish this book for a few years, but I thought it appropriate to mention this here.

And I was glad that the munificent nature of these universities toward its students did not encumber my salary. I was paid the handsome sum of 100 florins a year. It was still less than the law professors accrued, but definitely an improvement over the purse in Perugia.

Despite all these duties, I also continued working on my chess book for Isabella.

In short, I was busier than ever.

24,157,817

Chapter Thirty-Nine

THE WALL

I was almost too busy to notice that Italy had descended into warfare. King Louis XII and his French farts had invaded all the way down to Naples again. They attacked Pisa first with Florence's help, because of course everyone likes to throw stones once the game has begun.

Even artists were fighting each other. Leonardo moved onto yet another project, a large wall painting in the Palazzo Vecchio. It was going to be the largest mural ever completed. Given the current political climate I suggested Leonardo paint a scene from the Battle of Anghiari, the infamous battle I mentioned before where the man fell off his horse. The posturing and pointlessness of the current state of affairs seemed to need such a fitting tribute, although since the battle is known as a marker of Florentine dominance in the region, the Gonfaloniere was more than obliged to take Leonardo up on his surreptitious pitch.

But as I said, even the artists were against each other. Sensing he might draw more blood, the young and brusque

Michelangelo, who had already stolen the Giant commission from Leonardo (his words, not mine), not to be outdone, was able to convince the Gonfaloniere to give him the wall directly opposite Leonardo's, denying Leonardo the sole title of producing the largest mural and putting the two men in direct artistic competition against one another.

It was to be a Battle of the Brushes.

39,088,169

Chapter Forty

THE OUSTER

I secretly held a passion for the rivalry brewing between Leonardo and Michelangelo, curious to see which man's wall would come out on top.

But this passion held no match next to the intense dispassion I felt when I got word that Guidobaldo had been ousted as the Duke of Urbino. It wasn't the French that ousted him, though. Rather, it was Pope Alexander VI. Or, more precisely, the Pope's bastard son Cesare Borgia who was head of his armies. Even though Pope Alexander VI didn't legitimize his son, he gave him control of part of the papal territories. The Pope had Cesare conquer all of Romagna and Marche, including Urbino.

This meant that Guidobaldo, the shining light, the benevolent dictator, my dear friend, was no longer the duke. I was furious. I could feel my fists clench and shake. Was that the sound of the Patara? No, it was just a pounding in my ears, but I wished it were the clanging of the bell sounding the beginning of an opportunity to purge the feeling welling up inside me. Why would the pope do something like this? It was purely, blatantly militaristic.

I traveled to Rome, determined to confront Alexander VI, but found my forceful denunciation stunted by none other than my other friend Cardinal Guiliano della Rovere. I was just about to brush past his guards, thinking perhaps I would be like Leonardo and find something to throw at his head, when Guiliano grabbed me and bade me cool the tempers that hadn't come to a boil since before my novitiate.

"Don't go in there," Guiliano beseeched me. "Your problem will soon have no cause."

I should have asked Guiliano why he thought that, but I trusted him. I didn't ask for an explanation. I thought perhaps that there was a lot of militaristic movement, behind-the-scenes betrayal, and mistrust that I was not privy to which could explain his ouster, but that in the end perhaps nothing would come of it and everything would be restored to its former glory.

Nothing did end up coming of Leonardo and Michelangelo's battle after all. Michelangelo made preparatory drawings, but never started painting, having been called away to do the Sistine Chapel instead. Leonardo did finish his wall and I can attest to its splendor, but it went the way of his painting, *The Last Supper*, even faster than its predecessor. Unfortunately, Leonardo had invented a new bonding technique for his oil paint, but when the air became full of water after a rainstorm, Leonardo's invention couldn't set and his painting melted in front of his very eyes.

All that work and nothing to show for it, the hallmark of his and too many men's lives.

63,245,986

Chapter Forty-One

WHERE THERE'S SMOKE . . .

I was once again in St. Peter's Square waiting for a new pope to be announced. This time, though, my sidekick in such times was not beside me. Guiliano was in the conclave, voting on the man to elect as the new pontiff now that Pope Alexander VI was dead, having fallen ill shortly after Guiliano stopped me from confronting him.

Suddenly, the word echoed throughout the square, the new pontiff was Pope Pius III, formerly Francesco Todeschini Piccolomini.

Perhaps Pius III would restore Guidobaldo to his throne. I wanted to run up to the new Pontiff and plead his case, but I restrained myself. Guiliano would know when best to breach the subject with him.

After all, he had prophesied his ascension.

102,334,155

Chapter Forty-Two

THE RUMOR

A s I waited for the proper time to bring up the situation with Guidobaldo with the new pontiff, it seemed like many other esteemed members of the Papal order were falling ill. Cesare Borgia and Cardinal Adriano Castellesi both became housebound.

A rumor was circulating rapidly. There were often rumors of various kinds that I never took occasion to repeat, but this one seemed more important. I felt I must tell someone, but it couldn't be just anyone. I knew I had to take it to someone who could do something about it, should even a glimmer of it be true.

I went to Guiliano and told him the following: Pope Alexander VI and Cesare Borgia had wanted to poison Cardinal Adriano Castellesi, at whose home they were dining the night they all became ill, but they drank the poison themselves and that's why they were all ill now.

Guiliano didn't have the reaction I expected. When I first

heard the rumor my mouth was agape, amazed at hearing such a tale.

"I've heard that rumor, too," Guiliano said, smiling, before quickly concealing the corners of his mouth, even though I could still see a twinkle in his eye.

He must have been overcome with emotion, though, but he was resolute nonetheless. Guiliano told me to trust him. It was surely a rumor and nothing more. He promised me that together, we would make sure Guidobaldo would be reinstalled as duke.

The outlook, though, was less promising. It looked like Cesare Borgia and Cardinal Adriano Castellesi were both going to recover. While that outlook was good, and I prayed for their swift recovery, it also meant that Guidobaldo was less likely to be reinstated any time in the near future.

Pope Pius III had committed to working with Cesare Borgia, leaving him in charge of Urbino and reappointing him as head of the papal armies. I wanted to beseech Cesare, convince him that Guidobaldo was Urbino's true leader, but since Cesare wasn't fully recovered, it would have been unseemly to bring the subject up with him, a sentiment to which Guiliano readily agreed. I would never want to badger an ill man.

"I'll visit Cesare soon, though, and I'll make sure he's being taken care of," Guiliano reassured me.

I felt so lucky to have such a kind, thoughtful friend as Guiliano.

165,580,141

Chapter Forty-Three

TWENTY-SIX DAYS LATER

"What are the odds?"

These words were not only something I thought to myself, but words that I heard shouted, over and over again, at the bookies now overrunning the square. I had not seen them at the last papal conclaves, but maybe I wasn't paying close enough attention. What I could be sure of now, though, was that they desperately wanted me to pay them to bet on who would be elected the next pope.

I was in St. Peter's Square, again, waiting for the news of a new pope only a month hence from when the last one was announced. Pope Pius III, may he rest in peace, died only twenty-six days after being elected.

"Ten ducats on della Rovere!" a man shouted.

"I'm not taking any more bets on him. He's at eighty-two percent! He's basically a lock!" the bookie shouted back.

"But no one else has more than a six percent chance!" The bettor complained.

"Is it my job to help you win or is it my job to take your bet?"

Their exuberant exchange was engaging, due in no small part to the fact that they were discussing percentages with ease, but frightening, too. I felt as if I were in a dream (or was it a nightmare?) where I was forced to constantly relive this moment of my life, until such time as a new insight were to be made of it.

What I heard next didn't contribute to my feeling of reality.

"I announce to you a great joy—we have a pope! The Most Eminent and Reverend Lord, Lord Guiliano, Cardinal of the Holy Roman Church della Rovere, who takes to himself the name Julius II."

No, they couldn't have his name right. It's Guiliano? My Guiliano? A feeling of elation and confusion enveloped me like no other had before. I blinked my eyes rapidly, making sure they were seeing the same reality that the others around me were experiencing.

Seemingly, inexhaustibly, to make matters worse, what happened next really confused me.

Guiliano gave a speech, a rousing one, in which he declared, "Pope Alexander VI, a Borgia, a Spaniard, desecrated the Holy Church as no other before him." Guiliano stood there and spoke as if these were normal words to come out of the mouth of a pope. He stood there on the steps of His house, St. Peter's Basilica, and said, "Therefore, I will not live in any room where a Borgia lived. I forbid you speak or think the name Borgia again. I forbid it under pain of excommunication. They usurped papal power with the aid of the devil. Their memory must be forgotten, removed from every memorial, scratched out of every document. The reign of Alexander VI must be obliterated, all paintings of them, or indeed, all paintings they had commissioned, must be covered in black crepe."

Every pope must make his mark, undoubtedly, but these pronouncements seemed far out of line with this tradition and frankly, seemed more illogical than the Battle of the Stones. Why would he not even want to live where Pope Alexander VI had lived? Even if he hated the Borgias, as was surely becoming more obvious with every passing breath, Alexander's relatives had done Guiliano a favor, stripping his predecessor's apartment of nearly all its contents, in what was now practically a papal custom, including 100,000 ducats and the keys to the treasury. Perhaps though, these escapades did not endear the Borgias to Guiliano, as of course, they should not.

But if Guiliano's statements had surprised me, nothing could have prepared me for his final words, or perhaps not words, but rather, commandments.

"Open their tombs. Remove their bodies. Send them back to where they belong. Hell. Or, barring that, Spain."

267,914,296

Chapter Forty-Four

THE BETRAYAL

I had never heard Guiliano speak that way. I tried to approach him and discuss the matter, but his secretaries said he was too busy with papal business to be disturbed. I waited outside his chambers. After a short while he emerged and I tried to ask him why he had said those nasty things about the Borgias, but he cut me off.

"Don't worry, I haven't forgotten about you," Guiliano said before nodding and peeling off toward another one of his obligations.

While he didn't allow me to have words with him then, he did send a message, through the vessel of a messenger, that he'd seen to it that Guidobaldo will be given back control of Urbino, especially now, that is, since Cesare Borgia was in prison.

I should have been happy, but the Vatican was buzzing with rumors and this time I let them sting me. The rumor was that Guiliano met with Cesare Borgia, offering to keep him on as head of the papal armies in exchange for his support, for supporting Guiliano, that is, in the next papal election. But then after Guiliano was elected he had Gonzalo Fernández de Córdoba of Naples capture and imprison Cesare. Cesare thought Gonzalo and Guiliano were his allies, but they betrayed him.

I understood how he must feel. I was finding out so much about my friend Guiliano that I didn't know what to believe. Was he my ally, really? Another rumor told the story of Guiliano eleven years prior in 1492. He had almost been elected pope then, but lost to Rodrigo Borgia who, of course, took on the name Pope Alexander VI.

Apparently, Guiliano and Borgia had been battling it out during *Sede Vacante* along with the other Roman citizens. Guiliano had used Pope Innocent's illness, and more precisely the prolonged period it occupied, to form allegiances and gather support.

Borgia dispersed convoys of another sort around the city. As was the custom during the violent orgy that called itself *Sede Vacante*, rich men, cardinals, and any ordinary citizen with the means barricaded their homes out of fear of mob reprisal. Under the guise of this preparation, Rodrigo Borgia sent a caravan of four mules, all carrying silver, to Ascanio Sforza's palace. Borgia swore it was only to be kept safe from the hordes, but when *Sede Plena* came, Borgia's mind must have been elsewhere because he forgot to collect his treasure. How could his mind not be elsewhere? When the seat was filled, Borgia was in it.

After Guiliano's narrow loss, he and Borgia were enemies, so much so that Guiliano had to flee to France to escape the pope's wrath. There, Guiliano incited King Charles VIII to undertake his conquest of Italy, the same conquest that took place all those years ago at the same time my *Summa* came out. Instead of unlocking the secrets of my book, though, a generation of scholars had been lost on the killing fields, all due to the man I thought I once knew.

Regardless of how compelling these rumors were, and the evidence to support them was piling up daily, I knew I had to talk to Guiliano first before I could believe them. I needed him to tell me that they were all lies, that he was indeed, the man I knew him to be.

Luckily, I didn't have to wait outside his chambers to have this conversation with him, the reluctantly eager student hopeful to catch the professor, unaware that he may learn something truly transformative. Another messenger came to me to deliver the news. Pope Julius II wanted to apologize for ignoring me in the weeks after his election.

He wanted to invite me to dinner.

433,494,437

Chapter Forty-Five

JUST THE TWO OF US

There were no servants. Food had been left out for us. We would serve ourselves. It wasn't what I expected. It was just the two of us.

I had imagined it would be a grand occasion more befitting Guiliano's new position, but I was relieved, especially given the subject matter I wanted to discuss with him, that we would be leaving the pomp and circumstance behind and could pretend like we were simply two friends having dinner, and not a pope and his subject.

Even though he was my pope, though, I didn't hold back.

"Did you instigate the French to invade Italy?" I asked, beginning to unload all the accusations I had come across. "Did you poison Pope Alexander VI? Did you kill Pope Pius III too? I've heard so many stories. I just need to know that they're not all true."

I waited for my friend to clear all this up.

"I don't want to talk about any of that," Guiliano said. "I

want you to work for me, like how Alberti used to work for the pope, overseeing projects, weighing in on others."

"I don't know what to say," I uttered. I truly didn't. I felt my mouth fumbling with my answer, even though I didn't know what it would be.

"Say yes, we're both men of God and science. Your *Summa*, impressive. I want to put you in charge of the Vatican press. You won't just have to print ecclesiastical and religious texts, though, you can print anything you like. Distribute the wealth of our age to the people."

Now, I knew exactly what to say—yes! Of course I wanted to run the Vatican press, especially now that the narrow focus of its content would be lifted. It was the culmination of everything in my life that I'd been working toward.

My brain was screaming out *yes*, but another voice instead my head told me to keep that answer within me.

"I see it as part of my greater vision," Guiliano continued. "We need to take up the reins where other great men leave off and build upon their successes. I want to create a utopia of art, science, and religion. Perhaps like the one you experienced in Milan before it fell."

The small voice of restraint in my mind grew fainter until Guiliano spoke these next words.

"That was tragic. Ludovico should have been better prepared. You can't underestimate your enemies. You never know what they're doing, just lurking, building up their resources so that they can destroy you and everything you hold dear, just like the Borgias or the Turks did with Constantinople. Now, finally, we're going to be able to retake it and restore Christendom. I will unite all of Italy under one sword and then use it to cut off their bloody heads."

"All of Italy?" I asked, all of the food from our dinner suddenly hitting my stomach.

"I'll need to bring Venice under papal authority first. As long as those Turk-traders still enjoy autonomy, the other kingdoms will think they still have a shot at resisting my rule."

"And then what?"

"Bologna and Perugia, of course. And perhaps the University of Perugia will need a new dean. You're the perfect candidate, of course."

"And then what?"

"What do you mean, 'And then what?'" Guiliano shot back at me.

"I know people in Venice," I beseeched him. "I know people in Bologna, in Perugia. Good people, many of whom will die in the war you're describing."

"Many others have already died. We must avenge them."

What was briefly my greatest excitement had now become my greatest disappointment. His scheme seemed to have no end. His ambition and bloodlust larger than any cup could fill. I couldn't go to war with Guiliano—that was a foregone conclusion. But could I work for him now, knowing his ruthless intentions, knowing about his ruthless actions?

His vision was so beautiful, but I knew how many people would have to die for him to execute it. I could now intuit the answers to the questions I asked him at the beginning of the dinner. And I now knew better than to ask them of him again.

Guiliano must have sensed my reticence. He poured me a glass of wine and walked it over to me himself.

"You don't have to decide now, just think it over. Here. Have a drink," Guiliano offered.

I noticed he hadn't poured a glass for himself.

"Won't you drink with me?" I asked.

"No, please. Be my guest. I must get up early. No more long nights with you, my dear friend."

I chuckled at this, the happy memory of days gone by passing before my mind's eye, but I couldn't bring the glass to my lips. Guiliano had never sidestepped an opportunity to drink before. He was pope now, yes, and had the responsibilities that that entailed. But there were so many new things about him. He was so callous with life now. Would he get rid of me if I became inconvenient for him? Had I already become inconvenient? If the rumors about poisoning opponents were true, then I might be in real danger at that very moment.

"To our future together," Guiliano said, offering to toast me with my own water goblet.

But I no longer felt comfortable drinking wine out of a glass that Guiliano poured for me.

"Thank you for a lovely dinner," I said and started toward the door.

"What are you doing? What's going on?" Guiliano asked incredulously.

"I can't work for you," I answered. "And I don't think I can be your friend anymore either."

I turned and left the room. I wasn't trying to be brave or indignant, I simply didn't know any other way to behave. My dear friend had crossed a line so thoroughly that I had no choice but to make him a dear friend no more. Now, that I'd made my decision, though, would he make his?

Would he kill me to keep me quiet?

701,408,733

Chapter Forty-Six

THE REPRINT

I needed to leave Rome. Luckily, I had the perfect reason. I got a letter from Paganino, the printer who produced my *Summa* in Venice. Apparently there had been a slump in his overall sales and he wanted to reprint the *Summa* since it had been one of his best sellers.

I traveled to Venice to supervise the printing. I arrived ready to hunker down in his offices for another long printing run, but found out that Paganino only wanted to reprint the section on double-entry bookkeeping. Under different circumstances, I might have said no, but the reason that Paganino needed money was due in no short order to the policies of my old friend the pope. I thought he was going to open up the presses, but in practice, Pope Julius II seemed to be doing the opposite. He had made Paganino destroy a whole printing.

Paganino had printed the first edition of the Quran using Arabic characters. Guiliano ordered the whole printing burned. It wasn't until then that I knew how vehemently Guiliano hated

Muslims, how deep his hurt was, and how strong his resolve was to destroy them.

Did he also hate the elegant numbers they had given us? Or the game of chess, so like the game he was now launching into? Did he hate that? Chess was invented by the Arabs around the same time as Mohammed. If it were not for the spread of Islam, we might not have heard of the game. If he saw Ibn al-Haytham, whose work in optics stood next to Brunelleschi's in linear algebra . . . If he stood before that brilliant man, one among many who pushed my field forward, would he spit in his face? Would he chop off his head, as he previously intoned?

Islam believes in God. They do not worship any other. They follow the teachings of Jesus. They follow the prophets Abraham, Adam, and Moses. How are they our enemies to the extreme that we would destroy their religious texts? While I may not agree that theirs is the final version of God's prophesy, I do not hate them for trying to connect to God's plan. Such is my life's work as well.

Suffice to say, upon hearing Paganino's horrible news, I readily agreed to the reprint on whatever terms Paganino wanted.

1,134,903,170

Chapter Forty-Seven

ON THE GAME OF CHESS

Of course, my little stand could only do so much. Pope Julius II, as I now shall call him, the Guiliano I knew seeming a different person and one who I was no longer on an intimate level with, conquered Bologna and Perugia, just like he said he would.

I finished my *Schifanoia* as Pope Julius II was moving his pawns across Italy. I dedicated the tome to Isabella d'Este, the chess prodigy and its patron. Even though I knew Pope Julius II's next target was Venice, I stayed in the city to supervise the printing of this book. I also stayed because, although I abhorred having any knowledge of the subject, I knew that the pope didn't have the military power to fight Venice on his own. So, I was safe, at least for the time being.

After my *Schifanoia* became available, I started finishing work on my *De divina proportione*, the project I started all those years with Leonardo. Unfortunately, although Paganino's business was doing better, and the fact that his increase in business was almost entirely related to the double-entry-only reprint of my *Summa*, he let me know that he wouldn't have enough money to finance the publication of my *Divina* when I was finished with it, which would be soon.

It seemed the Venetian spirit, though, had something else in store for me.

As was perhaps too often the case, I passed a group of drunk painters jumping into the canals one night. I knew they were painters because I had met some of them before as friends of the artist Bellini. It all seemed perfectly harmless fun, the type that Antonio Cornaro and I used to get into, until one of the men jumped into the water, but then didn't come up!

"Does anyone know if he could swim?" one of them asked.

"He's German, so probably not," another answered.

I could feel my body tensing up. With each passing moment I started to feel as out of breath as the man in the water surely was.

"Now's not the time to debate this," I bellowed, jumping into the water to save the gentlemen since it seemed his friends wouldn't. Luckily, they did help me drag the man out of the water. In my advanced age I don't think I could have accomplished that task on my own.

After a swift punch to the gut, the man coughed up the brackish canal water inhabiting his lungs. He continued coughing, hacking loudly, until his fit turned into that of laughter.

"I was warned not to feast with painters," the man cackled. "I'm glad I paid them no heed."

I followed the revelers as they hoisted the nearly drowned man into their arms and took him back to the home of the German merchant in which he was staying. While he continued coughing up the last remnants of canal water, I chatted with his host. This merchant fellow had known Rompiasi, my old master. Apparently, the nearly drowned man, whose name was Albrecht Dürer, was doing something similar for the merchant. Apparently, Dürer was already becoming well known for his high-quality intarsia woodcut prints.

To my surprise, Dürer recognized me. In addition to his woodcut prints, he'd been studying perspective. He'd been in correspondence with Leonardo da Vinci who introduced him to my work. To my embarrassment, Dürer began listing my various accomplishments and assorted written materials in front of his host, who nodded along, although I was sure he was only doing so out of a modicum of respect.

At the end of this obsequious litany, I said, "All that and no one will finance my next book," trying to couch his praise.

"That can't be true!" Dürer said, almost as out of breath as he had been in the water.

"Of course, it's not true," the German merchant said. "He's just found a new patron."

1,836,311,903

Chapter Forty-Eight

THE QUANTITATIVE STRENGTH

Indeed, that German merchant did finance the publication of my *Divina* when it was finished. Perhaps I should stop referring to him as that German merchant, though, since he did have a name and it was, fittingly, Hertz, meaning big-hearted.

Although Leonardo and I had fallen out of touch and he didn't have a hand in writing my *Divina* with me, I rekindled our partnership in order to have him to render the drawings of the various skeletonic solids for that section. It was a task more arduous to get Leonardo to finish the drawings, though, than it was for me to write the book, but I was happy with the outcome nonetheless.

Then, as soon as I'd finished the manuscript, but before it went to print, in the complete reverse to what normally happened in my lifetime, I found out that my dear Guidobaldo had died from gout. He was only thirty-six, still in the prime of his life. For this reason, his death hit me particularly hard. Guidobaldo inspired me on my journey.

In the back of my mind, I was always doing research and writing my books directly for him, as a symbol of his generation. Normally I would have gone to Urbino for his funeral, visited the library, and reminisced about our good times there, but every time I thought about doing that my eyes welled up with tears and I had to tuck myself into an early bedtime. It seems the dam in my eyes that holds back my tears has become less firm with age.

And besides, it wasn't safe to travel the roads then anyway. You'd have to fight your way past an army. The world was ending, or so it seemed. Pope Julius II encouraged Emperor Maximilian of the Holy Roman Empire to attack Venice. The city was under siege. Music no longer filled the streets. The sweet smell of incense was gone.

I fought the siege the best way I knew how: I wrote another book, *De viribus quantitatis* (*The quantitative strength*). I hoped it would, in my way, show the qualitative value of my strength. It was a treatise on mathematics and magic, in some ways, a combination of my *Summa* and my *Schifanoia*—in spirit that is, not in content. Instead of being focused on mathematical doctrine like my *Summa*, it focused on the practical applications of mathematical operations. It was the first book to dissect the magic of card tricks. It also teaches people how to juggle, how to wash their hands in molten lead, eat fire, make coins and eggs dance, and many other such things as might make a person popular at a party. Last but not least, it also includes the explanation of magic squares.

Similar to Fibonacci numbers, the numbers in a magic square add up in sequence, but in every direction instead of strictly linearly. It's a magic trick if I ever saw one, but as a mathematician, I might be particularly biased towards it.

Although you should definitely peruse my *Viribus* if you haven't already, I can't help but communicate the following tricks to you.

For the washing of hands in molten lead, one needs to soak one's hands in cool well water for a good long while, shake them briskly and then place them directly in to the molten lead. Don't worry, as long as you've followed these instructions precisely, the lead will not singe you. Also, if you can, put some grounded rock alum in it—the water, that is, and not the molten lead. It will be a miracle, at least to those who have not taken it upon themselves to be educated in the trick.

To prepare the illusion of a coin raising and lowering by itself in a glass, rub some magnetic powder on a copper coin and then place the coin in some vinegar. Keep some magnetic powder between your fingers, specifically your index finger and thumb. Place it against the end of the glass toward the location of the coin. As you move your fingers, your audience will be amazed to see the coin follow your fingers, like a duckling following its mother.

In a similar vein, one can make an egg appear as if were walking across a table by—out of sight of any onlookers—making a small hole in an egg, preferably with a pin, emptying it, and then replacing the egg's yolk with white wax, covering the hole you created and securing the illusion. Try to find a particularly long-haired woman and conspire with her to allow you to pluck one hair from her head. Once you've procured this strand of hair, fasten it to the egg with wax. Locate the other end of the strand and connect it to your finger using another small dollop of wax. You could do it with any of your fingers, but I prefer my middle one. Then, once you've done all this and the egg is in the middle of a table in front of your audience, you can move the egg around on the table. Hopefully, you'll add some artistry to these instructions and not make it so obvious that the movement of your finger directly relates to the movement of the egg, but such a level of direction is hard to go into here. I suggest practicing on your own and in front of a friend. Although your biggest friend in this trick will be to do it in a location that's as dim as your audience. It must not be too brightly lit and you should keep your audience a short distance from the table.

While I was writing my *Viribus* I would often receive the most curious encouragement from my friends. And although I could consider it encouragement, it was most often in the form of a directive. It was not uncommon for people to be burned at the stake for witchcraft, as absurd as that notion is, and my friends counseled me not to make too much a public display of my work, as such an endeavor might draw the wrong type of scrutiny. But this, my dear reader, was exactly the goal of not only my *Viribus*, but of my life's work, the demystification of those otherwise seemingly supernatural elements and shedding proper light on them. I needed to prove that some of the actions that caused people to be burned were nothing more than the sleight of the hand, or the implementation of knowledge beyond what was commonly known.

I feel the need to correct some of my last words, those that seem to imply that these practitioners had caused their own burning and it was not the dull, fearful minds of some in their audience that were responsible. This was wrong and I apologize to these souls who were lost due only to the ignorance of others.

A second section of my *Viribus* was dedicated to equations and games showcasing mathematical operations. The purpose of this was to inculcate the practical application of mathematical doctrines by having a bit of fun with them, and showing that you might be able to apply them to your daily life, albeit in a sometimes more hypothetical fashion.

I almost hesitate to mention it here since, in retrospect, it may not coalesce with other statements I've given hereto on the importance of inter-religious harmony, but I will share this with you nonetheless, because it's such a clear, and to me silly but intriguing, model of how a clear grasp of mathematics could potentially save your life.

Let's say you're on a ship in a stormy sea, and the only way to save some of the men's lives is to throw a few of them overboard, at least enough so that the ship does not sink or capsize. How do you make such a determination? Surely volunteers would be the first to go, but assuming there are none, or at least not enough to bring the ship out of peril, some sort of just determination should be made in order to decide whose lot would be unlucky.

Mathematics, being an impartial judge of men, could, in this case, be employed to make a selection no man would dare otherwise. At least most men wouldn't. Although now that I say even that, I find the words a bit suspect.

Regardless, let's say you are on the ship with thirty Jews and one other Christian, so thirty Jews and two Christians in total. And let's say everyone arranges themselves in a perfect cir-cle (although *perfect* is perhaps the wrong word for this type of ghastly circle) under the guise that you will count around the circle by an interval of nine, throwing each man overboard who happens to be in the ill-fated spot, until the ship is out of dan-ger. Using mathematics, how could you not only increase your chances, but ensure that you would never be selected?

The first step in this endeavor would be to stand next to your Christian brother, assuming you wanted to share your good fate with him. The second and most important step, however, would be to arrange yourselves so that you were five places to the right of the beginning of the count, assuming it proceeds in a counter-clockwise motion. Since it's a circle, you could flip these instructions if the count is to be made clockwise. This way, no matter how many men are thrown overboard, you and your Christian brother would escape the tempest of God's wrath, at least for the time being, being the last two men on the ship.

So now, I'm sure that you can see why I was initially hesitant to relay this problem—this game is too similar to the one Pope Julius II was playing, his Jews being Arabs and other Italians. And he didn't need the impetus of a storm to instigate the game.

Perhaps now would be a good time to talk about my motivation for the producing this book. I believed, as did so many other great men around me in my life, in the importance of finding natural causes for supernatural phenomena. I was steadfast in my belief, though, that in finding the natural cause, I was, indeed, discovering the divine one, as He is responsible for all things natural. If one does not know His way, and perhaps there would be many such men amongst the Godless tricksters would might naturally be inclined to read a book like this, then perhaps they would also be inclined to learn more about mathematics, and as such, more about the divine magic of His creation through its explanations and mysteries.

More than explaining any one thing, though, or enlightening readers for a determined purpose, I wanted to bring back some of the light in the world that had been extinguished by Guidobaldo's departure. In this way, I returned to my old habit, yet one that I wished I did not possess. It seems like someone I love must die before I can give birth to something new. While painful, it did cement my reasoning for writing these books and perhaps this one as well: for if the world loses a great man, I must inspire another to take his place.

2,971,215,073

Chapter Forty-Nine

THE VITRUVIAN MAN

Venice rejoiced when it was announced that Emperor Maximilian's army was turning back, having failed at their attempt to conquer their city. The sea had been trying to conquer Venice for hundreds of years, though, so in retrospect, little Maxy stood no chance.

Now that the roads were open, I received a letter from Leonardo. He said he had figured out the solution to the Vitruvian Man. Had he really solved it? Had he really solved the puzzle that all the great minds after Vitriuvius had failed to solve? My feet danced on the floor as I read his solution. I knew Leonardo to be a great mind, but his discovery surprised even me. Perhaps it was only surprising to me since I had a mind that could move on after being stumped, whereas Leonardo would become fixated and toil away on things beyond his grasp, with the hope of extending it.

His solution was thus: You can't connect the corners of the square to the circle. Rather, only the bottom of the circle and square need to connect in order to create a diagram that fulfills Vitruvius's proportions. That question that he and I, and countless others, began trying to answer all those years ago, was finally solved. To prove it, Leonardo sent me a copy of his Vitruvian Man, a funny little sketch of a man that looks like he's being tortured as much as he'd uncovered the secrets of God and the universe.

I saw the divine proportion in it. The navel is a point of divine proportion between the hairline and the feet. The base of the hand is the divine proportion between the elbow and the fingertips. It was in the collar bone, the pectoral nipples, the distance from the elbow, the base of the hand, and to the fingertips. Although Leonardo and I disagreed on the source of the inspiration, I'm sure we could both agree that it was miraculous, both the ratio itself and his uncovering of Vitruvius's true intentions.

At least it should have been. It did uncover Vitruvius's intentions, but on closer inspection I discovered that the drawing itself did not precisely align with the divine proportion. It aligned, instead, with an approximate integer fraction of the divine proportion. Most of the time, one did not need to calculate the divine proportion precisely, and could instead rely on using very good integer fractions of this irrational number, since calculating it precisely every time you needed to use it would be an irrational endeavor on its own.

I sent Leonardo a letter congratulating him on his discovery. For the time being, I did not mention that I noticed he used integer fractions instead of the divine proportion, knowing that such a correction, at least to someone of Leonardo's temperament, was best left to be communicated in person.

$$4,807,526,976$$

Chapter Fifty

PROPORTION AND PROPORTIONALITY

Leonardo's letter was the signal I needed to push toward something I already knew to be true. I couldn't sit on my *Divina*, letting its release be the beginning of the end of its story. I needed to get out in the world and tout it, preach it to those who were willing to hear its message and convince the skeptics who would be content to let it slip away into a forgotten corner of a library. Vitruvius was proof enough that you must shout your ideas to every passing boat or else you'd have to wait until the next Leonardo to come to port and uncover your secrets, and even then you'd have to pray that he would be willing to take up the mantle for you instead of just keeping your knowledge to himself. I had to be the originator *and* the disseminator of my work. The printing press was my ally, but an ally cannot be counted on to maintain your kingdom.

I knew I needed to stand before a crowd and persuade them to take a chance on a tome that they might otherwise brush off, because they found the cover too off-putting or the language therein too stuffy. I needed to illuminate the knowledge within the book, and inspire them to plow through sections that might otherwise seem off-putting. I needed to get them excited for the *Divina* before I took it to the printer.

To accomplish that, I knew I needed to give a public lecture on its main theories, emphasizing the relationship of proportion to religion, medicine, architecture, printing, sculpture, music, law, and grammar. "Proportion and Proportionality" seemed like a good name for a lecture, an allusion to Euclid for those in the know, and I asked my friend Antonio Cornaro to spread the word that it was going to be a great event in order to entice all of Venice's dignitaries to attend, since he was still far more connected than I was to the social core of the city.

Now, as you may remember, public speaking and I were never on good terms. Dare I say we were never even on cordial or indifferent terms. So deciding to perform a public lecture to tout my *Divina* came as no small decision. Even as I prepared, I started to sweat and feel my throat close up, the affliction of my youth seemingly the affliction of my old age as well. But I continued preparing nonetheless—this information was more important than my personal comfort.

I began the lecture by noting the title's reference to the fifth book of Euclid. Then I started drawing the divine proportion using a compass, tracing arcs and describing the divine proportion for those who were unfamiliar to the basic concept of what I was talking about. But no sooner had I drawn my first arc than I drew my first heckler.

"So! You draw one arc and you think yourself Euclid?" The man yelled. I could tell the man was Dutch, if not for his accent then at least for his general demeanor. What I couldn't tell was the man's name. Surprisingly, Antonio knew the man well, or at least well enough to deliver the following rebuke.

"Shut up, Erasmus!" Antonio bellowed, leaping up from his chair.

Indeed, my heckler was the Dutch philosopher Erasmus, who despite being a classical scholar, often seemed to be quite unconventional in this manner.

"If I did consider myself Euclid it surely would have sped up the translations I've been preparing of his work," I said, hoping to keep the attention of the audience focused on my words and not the vulgar display before them.

"While I prepared my *Divina*," I continued, "I've also been working on two translations of Euclid, one in Latin and one in Italian."

I hoped this might ingratiate myself to Erasmus and end his onslaught, but as I soon would learn, that was not the case.

"It seems like you need to do better research," Erasmus interrupted. "There's already a Latin translation, and true scholars will always want to study Euclid in Greek or Latin. So, doing an Italian version is just wasting your time, as you are wasting our time today."

Now, I could have come to my own defense, but luckily, I didn't need to. A couple of other prominent members in the crowd did it for me. I had shown my new Euclid translations to Daniele Caetani and Francesco Massario, two noblemen and scholars whose opinions I trusted on such matters, and both men seemed as eager to talk over one another as they were to avenge me and cure Erasmus of his ignorance.

"The science of mathematics, after being hidden in speculation and conjecture, what was not practical because so many of the bodies had been reduced to various and complex figures, Luca's translation has rendered simple by explanation, so that even the very ignorant could understand just as if he had set it forth under their very eyes," Caetani said, his speech overlapping with Massario who gave a bit more than his two cents, something much more valuable than money could ever be.

"In this age of ours," Massario orated, "Master Luca Pacioli, Professor of Sacred Theology, with great effort, industry and care, has not only amended the text, but also added many things brilliantly devised for the elucidation of Euclid. Without the shadow of doubt, in this way he has returned Euclid to his true sense."

At that I thought Massario was done, but perhaps to rankle Erasmus even further, he continued, "In our times, Master Pacioli ranks before the rest. And to speak truly, he is the only true Phoenix."

This seemed to have the intended consequence because Erasmus seemed particularly perturbed by this last comment.

"The only true Phoenix?" he asked, as much to the heavens as to anyone in particular, before turning directly toward me. "In that case, your withered form looks like it must be approaching the end of its regenerative cycle. And in that regard, I hope you burst into flames."

There were a few gasps from the audience.

"What could you add to Euclid?" Erasmus asked, challenging me to respond.

Normally, my mind would have been screaming out in anger at his churlishness, but the degree to which others had come to my rescue seemed to have a great calming effect on my demeanor, to a degree I would not otherwise have been able to achieve myself.

"I have carefully digested Euclid," I said, as calmly as I could, with no venom or disquietude in my voice. "And I have added many notes of my own which may throw light on some of the more obscure passages, either in Euclid himself or in the translation by Campanus, the Latin one you mentioned."

Erasmus, always up for a fight, seemed put off guard by my serenity. And that's when I decided to strike.

"I originally intended only to produce an Italian translation, but knowing that some scholars will only want to read Euclid in Latin," I said before turning to the audience and truly leaning into the connotation of my next words. "I decided to produce a Latin version as well, so that these scholars may be brought up to speed with the students I teach in Italian."

There was enough laughter from the crowd to choke down any response Erasmus might have had. To my relief, Erasmus marched out, embarrassed, the red in his cheek as vibrant as the color he must have seen earlier, and I finished my lecture unmolested.

At this, our verbal exchange was over, but my mind had only just begun devising rebukes even more wretched than that one. Because I am a man of God, I will not share any of them with you now, but I would like to share with you something from my *Divina* that I wished I had shared, in all earnestness, with Erasmus.

As my *Divina* was written under the auspices of being useful for all mankind, my greatest hope is that it is accessible to everyone. I want it to be accessible so that if a person were to aspire to the understanding of art, science, or truthfully any profession, that they may be able to drink from its fountain, that fountain from which the streams of His knowledge flow. I would have jumped at the chance to relay this to Erasmus in the moment, for I truly believe that if a man were to heed this steady cry, then his mind will leap beyond the stars, instead of being bounded by them.

7,778,742,049

Chapter Fifty-One

THE PRINTING PRESSURE

Unfortunately, even though Erasmus was quite the worthy foe, the biggest hurdle I faced going into production was whether or not, at the end of the day, my book and the printing press it was printed on would actually exist.

The French were about to invade Venice just as the printing was going underway. The French had received support from Emperor Maximilian and Pope Julius II to take the city, their singular armies having failed or being inadequate to accomplish the task themselves. But now they formed a coalition, the League of Cambrai as they called it, although such a name does not represent the inherent vileness of their union, an unholy union if there ever was one, of France, Spain, and Ferrara along with Pope Julius II and the Holy Roman Empire.

I had fled Milan when the French invaded in 1499, but if I left Venice now both my *Divina* and my Euclid translations would not be truly finished. I had to stay and I made a vow to myself and to God that I would remain in Venice until the books were printed, even if I had to linger in an unholy realm after death and occupy some pliable soul until the work was complete.

I attended to the printing just as diligently as I had done in 1494 for my *Summa*. The only differences between these two periods were my now-advanced age and the fact that there was an active war going on. I again slept at the printing shop, not wanting to get caught up in any spontaneous skirmishes. I needed to finish, and deep down I knew that even if there wasn't a war going on this might be my last chance to publish. Who knew, Pope Julius II might well choose to shut down Paganino once the city was conquered.

I had to finish.

I had to keep God before my eyes. To accomplish this spiritual task, along with the one before us, I never forgot to practice my morning meditation. Even though it occupied time that I could have otherwise used to prepare the work for the day, my mantra of contemplation were the holy verses, as quoted from my *Summa*, "Time is not wasted by religious meditation any more than wealth is lost by charity."

No matter how deeply the city descended into chaos, however, none of the turmoil seemed to be able to shake Paganino. He said he was too excited to be the printer responsible for printing the first book to illustrate the construction of roman capital letters to let anything else get his spirits down. Perhaps this would be an area of lesser interest to those outside our two professions, it being of particular regard to mathematicians as well since I based the construction of these letters on the sacred, beautiful geometry of the circle and the square. But since Paganino and I both shared in the excitement of the execution of this section, our mutual interest made for a relatively jovial working environment.

I toiled tirelessly, but happily, alongside Paganino. Long, happy days turned into long, happy nights and even happier dreams.

Seemingly to reward our efforts, just as we finished our first round of printing, the French were driven out of Venice.

12,586,269,025

Chapter Fifty-Two

THE MONASTERY

Although I had not participated in the war, I was aged by it. Or perhaps it was all those other accumulated years and battles I had put up with over the course of my life, but I was old, and I felt it.

Printing my *Divina* and Euclid translations took a lot out of me. I would have liked to go back to teaching or perhaps begin a lengthier lecture circuit to promote my *Divina*. I had been offered a position as head of the monastery in Sansepulcro, but I wasn't sure if I should take it.

It was the same monastery where I went to school when I was a boy and accepting the position would be a bit of a home-coming for me. Still, I wasn't sure what I should do. As was often the case, I implored Christ for his wisdom. What would He do in this circumstance? Lead a monastery, a potentially clear favorite, or continue to preach His gospel through the life's work He had given me?

To try and receive His answer, I tried to follow in His

footsteps. That is, I went to the Pilate stairs in Rome, the same stairs that Christ had hiked up to His trial. The stairs themselves had been brought from Jerusalem 100 years before by St. Helen and placed in the Scala Sancta in St. John Lateran.

I didn't want Pope Julius II to know of my visit so I did not alert him that I was coming. Luckily, friars visiting Rome was an all-too-common sight and I could roam the city without worry of being discovered spontaneously.

When I arrived at the stairs, I found I was not the only traveler seeking solace in Christ's footsteps. I came across an eager young Augustinian monk from Erfurt in Germany piously performing an "Our Father" on every step.

"Who are you trying to get out of Purgatory?" I interrupted, my increasing age seeing no reason why my query should wait until he reached the top of the stairs and finished his indulgence.

"My grandfather Hans," he replied.

I started to turn away before he continued, lamenting, "I wish my parents were dead. And then I could gain indulgences for them too. I don't know when I'll ever come back here again."

These words struck me across the face. I wish my parents were dead . . . How perverted must this thinking be that one would wish ill upon his parents before their time has come. My parents were taken from me much too early in life. I would gladly have given my life in order for one of theirs to be spared instead. How foolish, how callous . . .

I could see on his face that he did not mean this statement impudently, but rather earnestly, ardently aspiring for his parents to achieve a place in paradise before their passing.

Unfortunately, in perhaps another example of my age taking priority over my courtesy, I launched into this poor, young monk with all the feelings of anger and disgust that his words unloaded within me, and not the empathy it should have. In retrospect, I don't know if Caetani and Massario would have been able to talk me down.

If I were a snake, I would have untethered all my venom in his neck. In reality, I got so close to him I'm sure some of my saliva ended up on his collar.

But my strike could hardly find a target. I berated his choice of words, but then quickly bore my fangs for the Church itself, at the system of indulgences the monk was, well, indulging in. I ranted about how perverted a system must be that would ever plant such a notion in a monk's mind. The whole system of buying and selling salvation was corrupt. You no longer need to follow in the footsteps and teachings of Christ in order to gain eternal life. You simply need to buy your way in. If Christ were to return, He would throw us out of His church as just another group of the merchants and money-chargers He threw out of the temple. I even brought into my argument a bit of Romans 1:17 for good measure.

I give you these words now, not as a means to record this diatribe as a legitimate attack of the Church, but rather to fully illustrate how far my arrow had flung passed its target. In retrospect, I was still feeling betrayed. I was angry at Pope Julius II, and that's why I also started complaining to this poor monk about the pope. Being a foreigner, he might not had have heard all the rumors about Pope Julius II's election and his rivalry with Borgia. Well, it pains me to say this, but I'm nothing if not a good educator so I took it upon myself as my mission to relay every single rumor I'd ever heard about Pope Julius II, even the ones I know had been falsely made.

I must have spoken for many minutes because my voice was becoming hoarse, almost as hoarse as it would have been after a particularly loquacious lecture, something in which I was now doubt currently occupied.

Luckily, I could feel the hate I was spewing leave my body. I saw this young man listening intently, eyes wide with forced focus, as one does to men of my age.

Of course, as soon as I realized what I was doing, and it was a long time at that, I immediately proceeded to apologize to this gentleman with all the energy I had left. My apology was profuse, and perhaps to some, potentially even more embarrassing than what I did to cause it.

To his credit, he was immeasurably gracious. I shall ever be indebted to his kindness, his understanding, and, well, for not making me feel as much of the tottering old fool as I had proved myself to be. I shall never forget that man. Martin Luther, I think, was his name. He was an Augustinian no doubt, I remember that part. In my attempt to make small talk with him in the denouement after my folly, he told me he was in town trying to get an exemption from the pope so that his monastery would not have to unite with some other Augustinian monasteries.

Well, I took it as a sign. How could I not? If this courteous young monk was the result of a monastery, and, well, all monks are I guess, I took it as a sign nonetheless: If I had come to the Pilate stairs in order to determine which path to take, Martin had surely been sent from God as an answer to my query.

I was initially hesitant that I might not be up to the task. Although I'm the head of the monastery, as you might be able to tell, since I have the time to dictate this tome, it is not a demanding job. I only have about six friars under my jurisdiction. It was an opportunity to slow down. I didn't have to decide this for myself, though, my body, now sixty-four years old, had made most of the decision for me.

Even though I was comfortable in my new life of leisure, I could not help but get excited when the painter Raphael came to visit and ask me a question. Would I come to Rome with him? He'd been hired by Pope Julius II, as part of the latter's rebuilding of St. Peter's Basilica, to paint a wall near or leading into the Sistine Chapel, depending on how you look at it. The commission wasn't as high profile as Michelangelo's, but he wanted to do a good job nonetheless. Raphael's plan was to paint the School of Athens, featuring the great thinkers of our time, inspired by the court in Milan that Leonardo and I were a part of.

While I turned down Raphael's entreaty to join him in Rome, my encounter with the monk being the surest sign of the danger of my unresolved emotions toward Pope Julius II, I did sit for Raphael for his painting. I wore a red cap with black trim, trying to recall the pose I had made for Piero all those years ago, the one that allowed me to be comfortable sitting for two days while he sketched me. But my body could not find a position that would reliably calm my aches for any extended period of time. Perhaps I even found the position that could have otherwise proved a hearty solution, but the body that found it was now decrepit.

But Raphael had not come to me merely to paint my likeness. Raphael wanted me to oversee the implementation of perspective in his new work. The artist learned perspective from Leonardo, so in a way, he was a student of mine as well. He as a capable student, though, and didn't need much guidance, having learned my lessons without me. I could have perhaps felt betrayed by this as no longer being needed, but instead I felt an immense feeling of pride, for this was exactly the type of exchange of knowledge I had long worked for. Knowing that I could not join him in Rome, I offered to work with Raphael on his sketch for the wall, an offer to which he readily agreed.

20,365,011,074

Chapter Fifty-Three

WILL AND TESTAMENT

It was a fever. His blood ran so hot already so I was surprised to learn that he died of a fever. I thought his body would have learned to adjust to his temperament. So, it was thusly that the reign of Pope Julius II came to an end. I could have then tried to catch up with Raphael, go to Rome, and help him with his wall, but such an endeavor was not necessary. Raphael had already gathered all the knowledge he needed from me.

Pope Julius II kept fighting until the end, so much so that Erasmus mocked his death, implying that Guiliano, even upon approaching St. Peter and reaching heaven, felt his reign would last as long as there was discord amongst the cardinals as to who would take the throne after him. That is, assuming that the extended della Rovere entourage left the throne behind when they ransacked his apartment. Of course, this last part is a joke. I only make it to you, my dear reader, to show you that as much as I despised Erasmus, or at least his temperament, I couldn't help but agree with his satire, at least in this regard.

This was to be expected of Pope Julius II, though. He had, after all, been the founder of the Pontifical Swiss Guard, a mercenary battalion ready for battle after he had seen them firsthand when Charles VIII invaded, at Guiliano's behest no less.

Near the end of his life, Pope Julius II had attached Florence and deposed Soderini at the whim of the Medici who bade that he be exiled to Dalmatia. I was heartbroken, not only at the departure of Soderini, a man who truly shepherded the administration of an amazing system of public education, among his many other duties, but by how swiftly those who served with him denounced his tenure as soon as it was over. Niccolo Machiavelli, once supremely loyal to Soderini's leadership, spoke out against him as soon as he was across the Adriatic. Unfortunately, loyalty often wanes with the moon. And how often do men chastise the old moon in order to gain favor with the new.

Another reason I didn't go to Rome was that I didn't want to be reminded of the good times I had had with Guiliano. Memories of joyful afternoons and exuberant evenings would have flooded my memory like the morning tide. Although we didn't end our relationship on good terms, I was sad to have lost my friend.

But in the end, loss comes to us all. I knew I needed to prepare a will for myself. As one might expect, I left my soul to Jesus Christ and His mother, the Virgin Mary. In His honor, I added a clause that one-third of any money from copyright infringement on my books will go to the poor.

Luckily, I saw that I was receiving some help in taking care of the world's poor. A new pontiff, Pope Leo X, formerly Giovanni di Lorenzo de Medici, inherited the papacy from Pope Julius II, but not his predecessor's worst qualities.

This came as a surprise to me, though, since Giovanni was

not ordained when he was elected Pope. Hopefully he would end up being more magnanimous than Guiliano, who had been made a cardinal before being ordained as well.

Although the French and Venice united to conquer and divide northern Italy amongst themselves, and who would have thought such a sentence was imaginable, Pope Leo X didn't fight them. He let them have their Battle of the Stones. He occupied himself in the fight for their souls.

This made him a man I thought I could work with.

32,951,280,099

Chapter Fifty-Four

THE LAST DAYS

Pope Leo X's ascension reinvigorated me, like the bear who lies dormant in his damp cave only to reemerge when there is more sun and light in the world.

I went back to teaching mathematics, on Pope Leo X's request, at the University of Rome, at the ripe old age of sixty-nine. I had him hire another mathematics professor to help me with the workload. Though I had reemerged, I was not a butterfly coming out from a chrysalis, but rather a fish who had been placed into a pail of water after spending an inordinate amount of time on dry land. Although there were now two professors in mathematics, there was still another in astrology since the university was still kowtowing to that demand. And that doesn't even begin to take into account the twenty in civil law, the eighteen in rhetoric, seventeen in philosophy and theology, fifteen in medicine, eleven in canon law, or the three professors in Greek. Nearly every area of study had more professors than that of our dear mathematics. We only had more professors than those students who were unfortunate enough, at least as far as professorial resources go, to study botany, which only had one professor.

I took on the role, either appointed or not, I can't remember, of elder statesman at the university. I also consulted on some of the pope's projects, just as Alberti had once done. Perhaps to continue on in that vein, in Alberti's shadow as much as I could, I lived at St. Pietro in Vincoli, the same place where I had lived with Alberti and Guiliano.

It was there that I had a bit of a reunion with Soderini, another exile from Pope Julius II's reign, whom Pope Leo X had taken in.

I loved strolling through the Vatican library, the same library I visited after Alberti died. It was a quiet place, one where I could read and write and sometimes, with voices lowered to the lowest of volumes to avoid disrupting the studies of scholars such as myself who wanted to explore the treasures of the library in peace and quiet, I would engage the esteemed men of the day, those minds that would have been invited to the School of Athens had it not already been dismantled. Those great men from various backgrounds, the architects like my Alberti, the painters like my Piero or Leonardo, the sculptors like Michelangelo, albeit generally less gruff and more genial, and musicians and teachers, like myself.

I was glad to be busy in this second life in Rome. Although I was happy to reminisce amongst the words of great men who had passed, in the halls where I had found important men after their death, I was glad to be alive and not dead.

When I die, I wondered, would others come here to try and find me?

53,316,291,173

Chapter Fifty-Five

THE DIVINE PROPORTIONS

I fear I must wrap up the story of my life, for we have now come to this present moment, as I lie on my death bed with a young friar transcribing my words.

If it feels like I have been speeding toward the end of this book, it is because I am reaching mine.

I am dying, but there is still breath in my lungs. I am hopeful that I may all of a sudden rise out of this bed and travel the countryside, hoping that the ideas I have laid forth in my books will be as ubiquitous as the chestnut tree. But I am confident that this will not happen. I may be a professor of mathematics, but I have learned the lessons of history as well. Old men die and I am old. My memory is fading. I have not given you specific years or dates for a lot of the events laid out in this book. Some are known to me and some have been lost in this old man's memory.

This period of my life is my last chapter here on earth. I wish that after my death I could tell you what lies on the other side to prepare you for that world, as I have tried to help prepare your minds in this one. I won't be able to, but even if I could, and really, I don't think I'd want to.

I have spent my whole life preparing for this moment, but I feel as if I have done nothing at all. I have done nothing that could possibly prepare me for what lies beyond. If I have not lost you yet in these ramblings of an old man, and hopefully I will still have time left in me to go over my words and clean them up, I thank you for your kindness. While I am happy to pass after a long life, hopefully well served, it still scares me.

So many times in my life I've lost someone close to me before I release a new work. Now that person is me. Like some of my work, I am a compendium of my experiences with men far greater than myself. God has given me a life far greater than I deserve.

But these are the times in which we live. More great men seem to walk the earth at this time than any other yet recorded. I have lived in a time where men from all walks of life, from the cobbler to the doctor, the merchant to the mercenary, have all, in their humble, or sometimes not so humble, areas of interest, tried to push the world forward, both for themselves and to create a better world for those that come after them. I do find it quite odd, though, that all these great minds seemed to emerge at this point in time. Rome, Venice, Florence, Milan, Urbino and a seemingly unending list of other Italian nation-states are all at war with each other in a never-ending cycle of violence where one can never quite tell who is on who else's side.

Apparently, though, I was not the only man to hear the siren song of the Battles of the Stones during their youth turn away from it, plugging their ears, preferring a battle of brains over one of brawn.

Unlike when I was growing up, anything is possible. And the world is becoming smaller. Christopher Columbus has found a new route to Asia due to the patronage of the Spanish Queen Isabella I of Castile and her husband, Ferdinand. To properly connect these two sides of the world, though, one must take proper accounting of the voyage itself. Perhaps that's why Isabella and Ferdinand sent an accountant along with Columbus, to ensure that the venture does not run aground, at least before reaching its intended destination. This burgeoning world must be shepherded by proper accounting, science, and mathematics.

Now it's up to you, my dear reader, to continue my work as I have done for others before me. May my teachings be accessible to you and everyone you know, for the praise and glory of God. In the years to come, some people may refer to the years surrounding my life as the apogee of human development, but we have merely been tilling the soil for you to grow.

Just as God can't be properly defined nor understood through words, so too the divine proportions can't be designated by any intelligible number nor by any rational quantity.

We mathematicians may call something like this that remains concealed and secret *irrational*, but as always, with the divine proportion, there is a hidden unity and force to the universe.

I believe I have set out in this book to explain the rationality of my life's work. And in that way, I've failed. A man's life and his reasons are irrational, too. There are no words or numbers to properly ascribe to it. I have told you my story so that you may understand. But I have played a trick on you, a game, because I have set out to make something understandable which cannot be. You may never fully understand my reasons, but I hope that I have inspired you to find your own.

Perhaps all of the small choices I've made in my life have

built up upon one another and created a discernible pattern, but I lack the perspective to see it for myself.

God has given us a beautiful set of divine proportions, a pattern of irrationality that unites us all.

86,267,571,272

Transcriber's note: Fra. Luca Pacioli told me that he had one more chapter for me to transcribe when I left his bedside last night, but he passed away before we could reconvene. As best as I can remember, these were his last words to me:

"I wish there was a grand narrative to my life. I wish everything I've experienced added up to something immense and grand, like the Fibonacci numbers I've had you include at the end of every chapter. Tomorrow, I'll tell you why I've had you do what must have seemed like a nonsensical delineation. But now, I must rest."

I found Fra. Luca Pacioli the next morning at his desk, having spent the night correcting errors in my transcript and adding a few small insights, having died the way he lived, rewriting his last book. I see no addendum at the end, though, so it looks like he didn't have time to give me the explanation he promised. I will journey to the Vatican Library to try to figure out the intention of his words so that this book may be finished and perhaps, with the pope's permission, place it in the library there as well.

Et quasi cursores vitai lampada tradunt . . . And as the runners pass the torch . . .

About the Author

W. A. W. Parker grew up Adam Parker, not knowing until he was twelve years old that his full name was William Adam Washburne Parker. Since this was a mouthful for a kid growing up in northeastern Montana, an area *The Washington Post* has dubbed "the middle of nowhere," he remained Adam Parker until he earned his first film credit, found out he would have been the nineteenth Adam Parker on IMDb, and was thus in need of a pen name.

Adam discovered a lot of himself in Luca Pacioli. Moving around as a kid, Adam always made sure the first friend he made in every town was his local library. He studied at Harvard primarily because it is home to the oldest library system in the United States. As Luca does, Adam found that he could travel the world by roaming the stacks.

The Divine Proportions of Luca Pacioli is Adam's first novel, but you'll be able to read his second novel soon—about 20th-century architect Pietro Belluschi.

The author would like to thank the following libraries that were instrumental in the creation of this novel:

The Los Angeles Central Library
The Getty Research Institute Library
The Los Angeles County Library
The University of Southern California Library
The University of California, Los Angeles Library
The Occidental College Library
The Santa Fe Springs City Library
The Orange Country Public Library
The Cerritos Public Library
The Glendale Public Library
The Beverly Hills Public Library
The Palos Verdes Library District
The Pasadena Public Library
The Long Beach Public Library

NOW AVAILABLE FROM THE MENTORIS PROJECT

America's Forgotten Founding Father
A Novel Based on the Life of Filippo Mazzei
by Rosanne Welch, PhD

A. P. Giannini—The People's Banker
by Francesca Valente

A Boxing Trainer's Journey
A Novel Based on the Life of Angelo Dundee
by Jonathan Brown

Building Heaven's Ceiling
A Novel Based on the Life of Filippo Brunelleschi
by Joe Cline

Building Wealth: From Shoeshine Boy to Real Estate Magnate
by Robert Barbera

Christopher Columbus: His Life and Discoveries
by Mario Di Giovanni

Dreams of Discovery
A Novel Based on the Life of the Explorer John Cabot
by Jule Selbo

The Faithful
A Novel Based on the Life of Giuseppe Verdi
by Collin Mitchell

Fermi's Gifts
A Novel Based on the Life of Enrico Fermi
by Kate Fuglei

First Among Equals
A Novel Based on the Life of Cosimo de' Medici
by Francesco Massaccesi

God's Messenger
The Astounding Achievements of Mother Cabrini
A Novel Based on the Life of Mother Frances X. Cabrini
by Nicole Gregory

Grace Notes
A Novel Based on the Life of Henry Mancini
by Stacia Raymond

Harvesting the American Dream
A Novel Based on the Life of Ernest Gallo
by Karen Richardson

Humble Servant of Truth
A Novel Based on the Life of Thomas Aquinas
by Margaret O'Reilly

Leonardo's Secret
A Novel Based on the Life of Leonardo da Vinci
by Peter David Myers

Little by Little We Won
A Novel Based on the Life of Angela Bambace
by Peg A. Lamphier, PhD

The Making of a Prince
A Novel Based on the Life of Niccolò Machiavelli
by Maurizio Marmorstein

Marconi and His Muses
A Novel Based on the Life of Guglielmo Marconi
by Pamela Winfrey

No Person Above the Law
A Novel Based on the Life of Judge John J. Sirica
by Cynthia Cooper

Ride Into the Sun
A Novel Based on the Life of Scipio Africanus
by Patric Verrone

Saving the Republic
A Novel Based on the Life of Marcus Cicero
by Eric D. Martin

Soldier, Diplomat, Archaeologist
A Novel Based on the Bold Life of Louis Palma di Cesnola
by Peg A. Lamphier, PhD

The Soul of a Child
A Novel Based on the Life of Maria Montessori
by Kate Fuglei

FUTURE TITLES FROM THE MENTORIS PROJECT

Relentless Visionary: A Biography about Alessandro Volta
Rita Levi-Montalcini, a Biography
and
Novels Based on the Lives of:
Amerigo Vespucci
Andrea Doria
Andrea Palladio
Antonin Scalia
Antonio Meucci
Artemisia Gentileschi
Buzzie Bavasi
Cesare Becaria
Father Eusebio Francisco Kino
Federico Fellini
Frank Capra
Galileo Galilei
Giuseppe Garibaldi
Guido d'Arezzo
Harry Warren
Laura Bassi
Leonardo Fibonacci
Maria Gaetana Agnesi
Peter Rodino
Pietro Belluschi
Saint Augustine of Hippo
Saint Francis of Assisi

For more information on these titles and
The Mentoris Project, please visit
www.mentorisproject.org

CPSIA information can be obtained
at www.ICGtesting.com
Printed in the USA
LVHW030142040121
675628LV00005B/171